THE NIGHT CALLER

Esther & Jack Enright Mystery
Book Two

David Field

SAPERE
BOOKS

THE NIGHT CALLER

Published by Sapere Books.

20 Windermere Drive, Leeds, England, LS17 7UZ,
United Kingdom

saperebooks.com

ISBN: 978-1-912546-55-8

Chapter 1

Helen Trenchard came restlessly awake with the uneasy feeling that something had just happened. Something bad. Or perhaps it was just the tail end of a bad dream, as her subconscious mind handed over to its conscious companion for another day shift. It also smelt as if she was in hospital again — that clinical, antiseptic carbolic sort of smell that she remembered from that dreadful time when her appendix had burst and she'd been rushed off to the London Hospital in Whitechapel from her place of work in Dalton's Department Store in Aldgate. Except that she didn't recall any smell of peppermint in the hospital, whereas this morning it was in her nostrils every time she took a breath.

She slipped out from under the covers and, since it was a sharp morning in early September, slid her feet into her fluffy bedroom slippers and then stood up, intending to walk to the bedroom windows and pull up the blinds from under which the sun was already beckoning her into her Sunday day off. What she saw made her stop in her tracks, then look around the room in sudden alarm before padding, awe-stricken, towards her mirrored dressing table.

All her most intimate garments were spread in wild disarray across the dressing table, as well as the floor around it. Chemises, drawers, corsets and petticoats were strewn everywhere. She tried to focus on what might have happened while she'd been in bed, in the belief that the bad feeling she'd woken up with had not been a mere dream, but all she could recall was a vague memory of being on a train journey somewhere.

She raised the blinds hastily, revealing a commanding view of Hackney's Victoria Park, and she squinted her eyes against the bright rays of the morning sun as she pushed the casement windows upwards to let in the fresh air. She looked back at the black marble mantle clock that had been part of her childhood, had been bequeathed to her when her father died, and now sat in pride of place on the shelf above the empty open fireplace. Eight-twenty or thereabouts. Then, in a moment of blind panic, she looked behind her, just in case. The burglar might still be in the house somewhere!

Wrapping a thick housecoat over her ankle-length nightgown and arming herself with a poker from the set in the fireplace, she tiptoed to the bedroom door and opened it slowly and carefully, wincing as it gave its usual creak. She peered cautiously out onto the landing, glancing first up the narrow staircase to the second floor, then down to the ground. There was no sign of anyone and no furtive noises, so, poker firmly at shoulder height, she crept up the staircase to the second floor hallway, cursing the creaks in the woodwork despite the carpet.

She opened the door to the second bedroom with a pounding heart and threw it back to its full extent, in case someone was hiding behind it. Then, satisfied that the room was empty, she crept across the bare floor and checked the catch on the casement window. It was firmly locked and there were no drainpipes on that external wall, so whoever had gained entry to the house during the night had not used that route. Slightly more encouraged, she performed a similar check on the spare room she used for storage, which, like the second bedroom, was empty.

Back on the first floor she examined the bathroom and lavatory for any sign of broken glass, then reminded herself that anyone choosing that means of entry would have needed to be a fairground midget. So, the intruder must have come by way of the front door. What might have been stolen from downstairs?

To Helen's considerable surprise, there appeared to be nothing missing from either the sitting room or the small drawing room that she used as an office of sorts for her correspondence. The valuable set of ceramic statuettes that she had painstakingly collected over the years appeared to have no gaps as they sat in pride of place on top of the sideboard in the sitting room and even her gold pen — an indulgent present to herself on attaining her thirty-fifth birthday only last year — was still there, at the side of the leather writing compendium in her office. There was also still some ten pounds or so left in her handbag at the side of the writing desk, which, so far as she could recall, was all that had been in there.

Bemused, she pushed open the kitchen door and slipped quietly through it into the scullery, expecting to find glass all over the floor, where the burglar had broken in by way of the glass panel in the door that overlooked the small narrow garden. But nothing appeared to be untoward and, after glancing quickly through the window to make sure that there was no-one left in the garden, she moved back into the kitchen and put the pan on to boil. A cup of hot sweet tea what was she needed now — along with some sort of assurance that she wasn't losing her reason.

Ten minutes later it occurred to her that whoever had rifled through her underclothes had probably been looking for jewellery and would almost certainly have found it had they bothered to open the half drawer on the top of the dressing table. There was not a great deal and nothing really valuable, but she hoped that she hadn't lost her late mother's wedding ring, or the love-charm bracelet given to her by a hopeful suitor when she was nineteen, who had died of consumption when she was twenty. She went back upstairs, more confidently this time, and sighed with relief when she opened the half drawer and found everything intact. Then she looked up and — for the first time — she saw the note.

Two notes, to be accurate, but on the same piece of paper, a large white one of the type used in offices. It had been easy to miss, during Helen's first horrified sight of the underwear explosion all over her dressing table, since whoever had attached it to the mirror with some sort of putty had then carelessly launched one of her petticoats half across the mirror itself.

In the centre of the paper was a warning of some sort, in capital letters that had either been printed on there, or added using one of those new-fangled typewriter things that Helen could never quite get the hang of. It read 'ONLY YOU CAN STOP THIS', with no indication of what 'this' might mean. Underneath, in an a near illegible and illiterate scrawl was a far more obscene message which made Helen suddenly feel very sick, making her race for the lavatory bowl.

Another half hour passed before she emerged from her front door in her best walking out attire of a burgundy suit with matching plumed bonnet and black high-laced boots. She closed the front door firmly behind her and before turning the key in the lock she examined both it and the surrounding woodwork with minute care. There was no sign of any attempt to force the heavy duty mortice lock and no tell-tale 'jemmy' marks on the surrounding door frame. And that was the extent of Helen's limited understanding of burglary techniques.

From memory she was aware of the location of a 'fixed point' uniformed police officer who was always on duty where her own road met Mare Street and she walked down in that direction, comforted by the presence of Sunday strollers crossing the road, some of them accompanied by children carrying kites, bats and balls, and even toy boats that they could float on the ornamental lake inside the park itself. Sure enough, after a short walk, the conical helmet came into view from a distance, atop the head of a reassuringly strapping six-footer who looked, to Helen, no older than her nephew Simon, but who smiled encouragingly as she walked up to him.

'Good day, constable. I'd like to report a burglar.'

'Certainly, madam. Name?'

'I didn't get his name.'

'No, I meant *your* name, madam.'

'Oh, sorry.' Helen laughed with embarrassment. 'You must forgive me, but it's been a bit of a shock. My name's Helen Trenchard and I live at number 64, down the road there.'

'Victoria Park Road?'

'That's right.'

'Silly question, perhaps, but is the burglar still on the premises?'

'No, I'm sure of that. I made a thorough search of the house, armed with a poker.'

'Not a wise move, a lady like yourself on her own, but there you go.'

Helen looked up at him enquiringly. 'I'm obviously not familiar with police procedure, constable, but shouldn't you be writing something down?'

'Not my job, madam. My job is to preserve the peace and apprehend malefactors who I see in the act of committing crimes. If you want something written down, you'll have to go to the police station.'

'And where might that be?'

'Just up Mare Street, where we're standing now. A few hundred yards up there, on your right, just past the ironmongers.'

With a heavy and somewhat theatrical sigh, Helen thanked the constable for his assistance and ten minutes later she had taken a seat in the front hall of the rather cramped local police station. Once the duty sergeant behind the front desk with the wire grille was able to leave his young assistant in charge of the comings and goings he joined Helen, taking the seat next to hers and extracting his notebook and pencil.

'Now then, a burglary, was it?'

'That's right — last night sometime.'

'The address?'

'64 Victoria Park Road.'

'You live there with your husband and family?'

'No, I live alone.'

'A big house for a lady living alone, if I may say so.'

'You may not. Do you want to discuss the burglary, or the right of women to live their lives without the control of a husband?'

'Tell me about the burglary. What was stolen?'

'Nothing, so far as I can tell.'

'Was there nothing worth stealing?'

'Plenty, but none of it was,' Helen replied with irritation.

'Then how do you know you've been burgled? Was a door broken down, or a window forced?'

'Neither of those things.'

'Then how...'

Helen took a deep breath. 'Whoever it was rifled through my lingerie drawer and left various items strewn around my bedroom.'

'Your *what* drawer, madam?'

'Lingerie — "unmentionables"?'

'Oh, them things.' The sergeant nodded with a slight blush. 'And how many of them got stolen?'

'None, so far as I can make out.'

'Got a lot of them, have you?'

'None of your damned business. But I don't think any were actually removed — just sort of messed about.'

The sergeant was doing his best to suppress a smirk, or perhaps laughter, as he persevered. 'So when this so-called burglar was "messing about" — your own phrase, madam — with your "unmentionables", did you get a good look at him?'

'No, I was asleep.'

'So how do you know it was a man?'

'I don't, obviously — I was just assuming.'

'And for that matter, how did you know it was a burglar?'

'Forgive me, sergeant, but I'm not in the habit of inviting people to rearrange my underwear drawer while I'm lying in bed.'

'Asleep,' the sergeant reminded her.

'That's right — asleep,' Helen confirmed as her ire began rising.

'So how do you know you weren't sleepwalking or something?'

Helen took several deep breaths before looking directly into the eyes of the clearly amused sergeant. 'Just so that there's no misunderstanding on my part, you're seriously suggesting that in my sleep I got out of bed, threw my underwear all over my bedroom, then went back to bed and forgot all about what I'd done?'

'I've heard of cases like that.'

'Well, whoever did this also left a note.'

'A "thank you" note, presumably?' the sergeant choked as the sheer humour of it all broke through the serious facade he'd been trying to maintain.

Helen went purple in the face with anger and rose to her feet.

'I would thank you for your assistance, but I don't think you gave me any. Perhaps I'll have your full and serious attention when the same man returns one dark night and slaughters me in my bed. Or perhaps I'll only dream *that* as well. Good day to you and thank you for precisely *nothing!*'

She stormed out of the police station to the fading sounds of the laughter of not just the sergeant, but the young constable who'd been listening through the wire grille. Muttering dark imprecations about the attitudes of men in positions of authority and the ineptitude of the Metropolitan Police in general, Helen all but kicked in her own front door, stormed upstairs and rearranged her lingerie drawer before she'd even changed out of her walking out clothes. Then she took her strewn undergarments downstairs and dropped them in the laundry basket. She took one final scowling look at the note on the dressing table mirror, allowed herself a couple of obscenities, then ripped it down, screwed it up and hurled it into the waste bin in the corner of her bedroom.

So much for her day off. But at least she had something to look forward to the following day. Another step on the road towards the equality of women in the workplace and another blow against the police idiots who'd given her such a humiliating time.

Chapter 2

'You simply *must* have the wedding at St. Margaret's,' Constance Enright insisted as her housemaid Alice distributed the coffee and petits-fours down the Sunday dinner table. 'Lucy was married there and the local vicar does *such* a lovely service. You remember Lucy's wedding of course, don't you, Esther? You can't seriously be thinking of anywhere else for your own wedding to Jackson, now *can* you?'

Esther was not about to argue, for several reasons. The first was that no-one ever argued with her future mother-in-law, not even her closest family members, and if Esther was shortly to become an Enright by marriage, then she should honour the family tradition. The second was that the only alternative that came to mind was a synagogue in Spitalfields and that would hardly satisfy the social sensitivities of Constance Enright.

There was a third, more vague, reason and it lay in the recent past. When Jack — as everyone except his pedantic mother called him — had first introduced Esther to his family, Constance Enright had seemed to entertain some doubts regarding the suitability of the match. That had been in the 'bad old days' when Jack had been one of many police constables in Whitechapel on the case of the man calling himself 'Jack the Ripper', who had murdered at least five prostitutes before Esther and Jack had discovered the killer's true identity and prevented any more deaths. In those early days Esther had been scraping together a living as a seamstress, taking 'outside' work from her adoptive father Isaac Rosen back to her room in a lodging house down the road from his business premises.

The murder of a fellow lodger and friend had led Esther into a search for her killer that had brought Esther and Jack together, but given Esther's relatively lowly status at that time, Constance had seemed to suspect that Esther was just a pretty girl 'on the make' who'd latched onto a naive young man from a comfortable middle-class background in rural Essex. In the horrified belief that Jack might be of the same opinion, Esther had broken off their rapidly developing relationship, leaving them both devastated. It had taken the wiles of Jack's sister Lucy to bring them back together, shortly after Jack had saved Esther from becoming 'the Ripper's' latest victim.

Isaac Rosen had died at approximately the same time and as an elderly widower with no children of his own he had bequeathed Esther the garment business, complete with premises, in which Esther had been living for the few months before Isaac's death. This had made her what Jack chose to call an 'heiress' to a small fortune and it might not just have been coincidence that once Esther's enhanced status had been announced, Constance Enright had a change of heart and was now eagerly contemplating the marriage of her older child, and only son, to a somewhat spirited young lady whose Jewish ancestry was the source of her dark beauty, rather than a ground for suspicion or racial prejudice.

'Have you given any thought to bridesmaids?' Constance enquired.

Jack shook his head. 'We don't even know where we're going to live, Mother.'

'Well you can't live *anywhere* together until you're married, can you?' his mother pointed out, 'so let's decide on the bridesmaids, shall we?'

It was all Esther could do to restrain herself from pointing out that since she was the bride to be the choice of bridesmaids ought to be hers. However, she had no living relatives other than a brother in the Army somewhere in North Africa and no female friends of the sort of whom Constance Enright might approve — only Jewish girls like herself who'd grown up in the increasingly sordid streets of Spitalfields — so she listened with resignation as her future mother-in-law rattled off the options.

'Of course, there's no shortage of nieces, thanks to my brother and sisters, but Lucy had rather hoped to be offered "the role", as she'd no doubt call it, given her theatrical interests. It's entirely a matter for you, Esther my dear, but since the wedding will presumably be sometime in June, you should waste no time in asking her.'

'We hadn't actually fixed the date, Mother,' Jack complained, only to be met with a dismissive wave of the hand from across the table.

'That will rather depend upon when the Reverend Black has a date free, will it not, since we've agreed that it will take place in St Margaret's?'

'*Did* we agree that?' Jack enquired as he turned to smile at Esther, who nodded.

'I think that might be best,' she agreed with a docile smile across the table at Constance.

'You see, dear?' Constance beamed triumphantly. 'Your wife to be displays *far* more common sense than you do. You should regard yourself as fortunate in making such a good match with a young lady who can make sure that your bootlaces are tied properly before you leave the house. And talking of bootlaces,' she added with a sidewise look at her brother-in-law, Percy, 'what exactly have you got Jackson involved in, now that he's working with you at Scotland Yard?'

Percy Enright sighed and put down his coffee cup. 'As I seem to be forever advising you, Constance, I'm not my nephew's keeper. He and I rarely even pass each other in the Yard's lengthy and numerous corridors these days, let alone work together. His working duties are entirely the responsibility of Chief Superintendent Morton, who allocates men to specific teams as and when the need arises.'

'You're only claiming that so as to avoid any responsibility for that time someone took a pot shot at him with a gun,' Constance insisted. 'I do hope that you'll use your senior rank to ensure that nothing like that ever happens again.'

'I'm only a Detective Sergeant,' Percy reminded her, 'and I get what men I'm given. I can't insist that Jack be allocated on a permanent basis to searching for stolen property, or checking on cab licences. And if the Chief Super wants Jack on burglaries then there's nothing I can do to stop him.'

'Is that what you're working on at present, Jackson — burglaries?' Constance enquired. Jack nodded with some reluctance. 'And burglars carry firearms, do they not?' she persevered. Jack nodded again as Esther slipped her hand into his under the tablecloth. 'Well,' Constance continued, 'I need hardly remind you that you'll shortly become a husband and no doubt, after that, a father. You owe it to your unborn children to take care that you live for long enough to marry the lovely Esther here. And talking of weddings, who's your best man going to be?'

Jack gave an ironic laugh. 'Funnily enough, since I became a police officer I seem to have run out of friends. The boys I grew up with around here treat me as if I joined the French Foreign Legion and the few I've encountered on my occasional trips back here cross the road when they see me, almost as if they've got guilty secrets they don't want me to learn about.'

Constance gave one of her all-too-familiar 'harrumphs' and turned to glare again at Percy. 'You see? I knew it was a mistake letting Jackson go to live with you when his father died. It's thanks to you that he joined the police force, where he risks his life on a daily basis, rather than pursuing the family insurance business. And thanks to you, he doesn't even have any friends left. The least you can do is to agree to be his best man.'

'I haven't been asked yet,' Percy pointed out, 'so how can you imply that I've in some way refused?'

'Well, Jackson?' Constance responded with a demanding look.

Jack sighed. 'As usual, Mother has taken care of things. I *was* going to ask, but I was a little reluctant. Will you be my best man, Uncle Percy?'

'Would that be lawful?' Percy enquired.

'I'll speak to the vicar about that,' Constance assured them. 'Now — where will you both live after you're married? We have plenty of spare rooms here.'

Jack and Esther had anticipated that and Jack gave his mother their pre-prepared excuse. 'My duties at the Yard require that I live within the Metropolitan boundaries, Mother. That's regulation and there's nothing I can do about that. But now that Esther's come into money, we can probably use it to buy a house, or perhaps a set of rooms somewhere in London itself.'

Constance sniffed. 'Have you begun looking yet? How much do these things cost?'

'We've not really had much time to look,' Esther explained, 'since Jack's working for seven days out of every nine and the people who specialise in selling and renting out houses are only open on weekdays and Saturdays, so we sometimes only have one day a week in which to look at potential houses and rooms. Even then, it's not always convenient for the people living in them to open their doors at weekends.'

'But have you not even settled on an area of London?' Constance persisted.

Jack came to Esther's rescue. 'That's determined by price, Mother. With the seven hundred or so that Esther got for the old business premises in Spitalfields, we could choose anything from a crumbling old converted warehouse in Whitechapel to a tiny two-room apartment in Mayfair that's so small you have to breathe in heavily before squeezing into the kitchen, which is also the living room.'

'I sincerely hope that you've seen the last of Whitechapel — or anywhere in that dreadful East End,' Constance sniffed.

Esther made a mental note that their final choice would have to be somewhere where the street address was acceptable, even if the house wasn't. Then she became aware that Constance was looking intently at her from across the dining table.

'When do you have to vacate that awful factory place where you're living at present?'

Esther winced inwardly at the description of proud old Isaac Rosen's bespoke tailoring enterprise as an 'awful factory', but managed a smile. 'October the first.'

'But presumably the new occupiers will require access sometime before that date, in order to measure up for carpet, curtains and suchlike?'

'I don't think so,' Esther replied uncertainly. 'The people who bought the premises are a property investment company and they're intending to lease the place out to some sort of commercial organisation. I'm not sure exactly what, but Mr Hemmingsworth — he's the man I'm dealing with from the property company — asked that I be there tomorrow, to meet a lady who may be their first tenant.'

'So where will you live between October and June?' Constance enquired and Esther braced herself for the inevitable campaign as she admitted that she hadn't yet given the matter a great deal of thought.

'Well, you clearly can't go back to one of those horrible lodging houses in the East End where all those killings take place, can you?'

'We caught the Ripper, Mother,' Jack reminded her, but he was wasting his breath.

'That's not quite the point, is it dear?' his mother replied. 'There are desperate characters on the loose all the time down there, as you yourself must realise from the somewhat grubby line of work you've chosen for yourself. Esther simply *must* come and live here. She can have Lucy's old room, at least until the day before the ceremony, since the bride and groom mustn't see each other on the morning of the wedding, until they meet up at the altar.'

'But then she'd need to take the train into work every day,' Jack objected.

His mother's eyebrows shot upwards in horror. 'You surely don't expect your bride to go to *work* for a living?' she protested. 'And what sort of work, exactly? Taking in sewing?'

'I do accounts work as well,' Esther interposed meekly, but there was no stopping the old matriarch once she got her teeth into something.

'Out of the question! And now let's adjourn to the sitting room while Alice clears the dinner table. Or perhaps you young people would prefer to take a turn in the garden? You too, Percy, if you intend to smoke that revolting pipe of yours.'

Out in the garden, Percy gave a loud and ironic chuckle as he lit his pipe, then gave a credible, and much practised, impersonation of his sister-in-law.

'So *that's* all "agreed", Jackson. You and Esther will get married in June, in St Margaret's, with me as best man and Lucy as bridesmaid. Esther will be living here until the night before the wedding and is forbidden to engage in anything as sordid as work. I'm *so* glad we got all that sorted out.'

Jack gave him a rude gesture and turned back to give Esther a consoling kiss.

Chapter 3

'You must be Mrs Trenchard.' Esther smiled as she opened the front door of the now empty former tailor's premises in Lamb Street, Spitalfields, to the lady in her mid-thirties wearing a smart business costume.

'*Miss* Trenchard,' Helen insisted as she smiled back. 'Did Mr Hemmingsworth advise you that I'd be calling?'

'He did indeed. Do please come in.'

As they walked slowly around the deserted ground floor that had once rattled to the sound of half a dozen sewing machines, but had recently only echoed to the muted Hebrew folk tunes that Isaac had hummed as he worked alone on the latest commissioned made to measure suit, while Esther laboured away at the accounts books on the other side of the dividing curtain, Helen Trenchard was mentally converting the large but now empty space into a busy office.

'I believe there's some living accommodation on the upper floors, plus storage rooms and a kitchen?' she enquired.

'That's right,' Esther confirmed. 'I'll show you up there, if you've seen enough down here. Then would you care for a cup of tea?'

'It looks as if you're still living here,' Helen commented as they waited for the pan to boil, seated across from each other at the kitchen table.

'Yes, as you saw for yourself, I have the room on the first floor — until October 1st, that is,' Esther confirmed. 'I'm afraid that the top floor still retains some reminders of the fire that almost destroyed the place during an anti-Semitic attack some years ago, from which I barely escaped with my life.'

'You've lived here for a few years?'

'On and off since I was fourteen and my parents were killed in that pleasure boat disaster on the Thames,' Esther explained. 'The Rosens were old family friends and they took me in and taught me all I know about the garment trade.'

'You're a seamstress?'

'Among other things. Towards the end, before Isaac Rosen died, I did his books.'

'Books of account?'

'Yes, those certainly. But also order books, textile stock records and so on.'

'Really?' Helen mused. 'Are you now looking for work by any chance? I could use an assistant with your skills.'

'Are you in the garment trade?

'No, although a good number of my members are and your background in that would be an additional bonus.'

'Members?' Esther enquired.

Helen nodded, then reached into her handbag and handed Esther a business card. '"The National Women's Labour Alliance," as you can see. I had very few of these cards printed until we had a permanent business address. When I take over this place I'll have more done and your first task — should you choose to take up my offer of employment — will be to find a low cost printing firm in this vicinity. You *will* come and work for me, won't you?'

Esther didn't require long to consider her options. If she played her cards right she could kill two of Constance Enright's birds with one stone.

'Would I be able to remain living here?'

Helen looked slightly doubtful for a brief moment before nodding. 'I had half intended living here myself. I need to move out of my present house, after ... well, let's just say that I could use the sale proceeds towards further establishing my new Alliance. But yes, if it means that you'd be available here all the time, you could remain living here. In addition, I could offer you a wage of ten shillings a week. It's not much, but hopefully I'll be able to increase it once the Alliance finds its feet. And of course, you'd have your living accommodation.'

'I feel obliged to advise you that I'll be getting married next June,' Esther said. 'I don't know where I'll be living then, but it'll have to be somewhere here in London, because of my fiancé's job, so depending upon where it is I could probably take a bus down here every day.'

'What's your husband's job?' Helen enquired.

'He's a detective constable with Scotland Yard,' Esther replied proudly.

'I'll try not to hold that against him,' Helen muttered. 'But yes, of course, you could travel to work every day — until the babies start arriving, that is.'

'We weren't planning on starting a family immediately,' Esther advised her.

Helen laughed bitterly. 'Very few women do, but that's what happens. And that's how men can dominate their lives. Either they're unable to work because they're burdened with annual childbirth, or if they can they're paid an insulting pittance in reward for long hours and the risk of getting dragged into dangerous machinery. That's what my new Alliance has been formed to put a stop to.'

'Sounds very worthwhile,' Esther enthused. 'I grew up around here and I've seen a good bit of the garment trade for myself. As you say, the women who work in it are open to exploitation.'

Helen nodded enthusiastically. 'Not just in the garment trade either, as you'll discover when you come to work for me. You *will*, won't you?'

'Did I not already say yes?' Esther replied with a broad smile. 'If not, then I'm happy to confirm that I will. It just so happens that I'm seeking to escape from a form of exploitation myself. But only verbal. And from my future mother-in-law.'

Chapter 4

Mabel Barker looked up apprehensively at the dark clouds sweeping in from the west as she quickened her pace up Station Road from her place of work as a refreshment assistant at Brockington's Cattle Yards in the centre of Luton, towards the cottage that came with the job. It was looking like rain and her washing was out.

She decided to get it in before entering the house and scuttled down the side path and into the laundry, where her washing basket was kept. From there it was only a few steps across the grass to her clothes line and as she felt the first few raindrops on her head and neck she began removing the pegs hurriedly as she passed down the line, throwing both pegs and dried clothing into the basket. Then she came to a gap she hadn't noticed in her hurry to avoid the impending downpour.

Her best blue underwear was missing from the line and in their place someone had pegged a large sheet of white paper. She only had the benefit of a local Board School education, but even she could read what was there in bold capital letters: 'DON'T JOIN THE OTHERS'. And above it, written much more crudely in pencil, was a far more threatening message which sent shivers down her spine.

Chapter 5

'I'm so glad you decided to come home for your wedding, Jackson.' The Reverend George Weston smiled as he poured out three glasses of sherry in the vicarage living room late one Saturday afternoon. 'You grew up here and although I wasn't the vicar in those days your mother tells me that you were a regular church-goer until your father died and you moved to London to live with your uncle. Now, or so your mother tells me, you're a police officer dedicated to doing good in this sinful world and it's always such a comfort to a man to have the support of a wife waiting at home.'

'Not necessarily waiting at home,' Esther replied, smiling through slightly gritted teeth at the man's studied niceness and condescending attitude. 'I'll most likely be working as well.'

'And what exactly is your chosen profession, Esther?' the vicar enquired.

'I work as the accounts manager of a new employment organisation,' she responded, only her eyes betraying — to those who knew her well — that dangerous ground was being crossed.

'Esther — that's a Jewish name, isn't it?'

'All Biblical names are Jewish, if you think about it,' Esther replied sweetly, preparing to engage in the familiar skirmish regarding the relative importance of the Old and New Testaments.

'Quite. I just wanted to make sure that you're committed to the concept of a Christian marriage.'

'I wouldn't be here otherwise,' she replied. 'And Jews get married too.'.

'Do you have Saturday June 9th free, by any chance?' Jack enquired quickly.

The vicar beamed as he delivered one of his flat jokes. 'Presumably that's the day you'd like your wedding and not an invitation to a garden party? I don't need to consult my diary to confirm that the date you have in mind would be available.'

'But presumably you're going to make a note of it anyway?' Esther insisted and the vicar smiled back at her deprecatingly as he extracted a small notebook and pencil from his jacket pocket and began to make the necessary note at the back of it.

'This is this year's diary, obviously,' he advised them, 'but once I get my diary for next year, I'll enter the booking. It's Miss Jacobs, isn't it?'

'Yes,' Esther confirmed stonily. 'Another Old Testament name, I'm afraid.'

'What about bridesmaids and best man?' the vicar continued undaunted. 'Have you chosen them?'

'They've been chosen for us, certainly,' Esther bristled slightly, 'so that's all in order.'

'I'll need a note of your chosen hymns to give to the organist, Mrs Bratton. There'll be a fee for her services, of course.'

'And yours?' Jack enquired.

'Naturally. You'll also need to make another appointment with me in the near future, in order that we may have the usual discussion about the seriousness and significance of matrimony and the life-long commitment that it involves.'

'We obviously thought about that before we agreed to get married,' Esther reminded him, 'and I'm well aware of the obligation to "love, honour and obey", although my obedience might be tested from time to time.'

'All the same,' the vicar insisted, 'it's traditional.'

The vicar decided that perhaps it was a good idea to bring this interview to an end, which he did with a few tried and tested platitudes, before ushering Jack and Esther to the front door of the vicarage, from which they set off down Church Lane for an early tea with Jack's mother.

'You were a bit rude to the vicar,' Jack chided gently. 'He only means the best for us.'

'I'm sorry, Jack,' Esther replied as she took his hand, 'but all that Church of England sugariness makes me glad I was taught religion by rabbis. He's about as convincing as dung from a rocking horse and clearly overawed by your mother, like everyone else in Barking, so far as I've been able to deduce.'

'I hope this new job of yours isn't giving you revolutionary ideas,' Jack muttered as they approached the house.

'I haven't even started the job yet, so how would I know?'

'Well, it's just that these emerging labour unions have a reputation for being a bit — well, a bit sort of seditious and anti-authority. We have an entire department at the Yard that keeps a close eye on what they're up to.'

'Like I said, I haven't started the job yet and the only person I've met so far is a middle-aged, middle-class lady who just wants to join with other women in making working life better for themselves. What could possibly be wrong with that?'

'Nothing, expressed in those terms,' Jack conceded. 'But some of the men's unions have been known to take on entire contingents of police officers, like that mob that caused a riot in Trafalgar Square a few years ago.'

'I'm sure that Helen Trenchard has nothing like that in mind,' Esther assured him. 'And if she does, I'll be certain to report back to you. Talking of reporting for duty, here we are, back at the family headquarters.'

Chapter 6

Annie Cudsworth realised that there was something wrong the minute she opened the door to her room in Bolton's Lodging House, round the corner from Shoreditch Station in Rivington Street. At the end of another fourteen hour day mending broken threads in the weaving factory that paid her a grudging six shillings a week, she was nevertheless not too exhausted to notice the faint smell of something sweet, reminiscent of pear drops. Nor could she fail to see that her few simple clothes were strewn all over the room and that the contents of her laundry basket had been tipped onto the floor.

Shaking with apprehension, she hung her only two dresses back on their hooks. As she did so she became aware of a piece of paper stuck to the side wall. 'DON'T JOIN UP' was printed clearly in its centre. She pulled it from the wall and there underneath, written with the remains of her only lipstick, was another message. The scrawled, misspelt writing was hard to read, but it contained a lewd message about her underwear, and when she turned her attention to the items that had been tipped from the laundry basket onto the floor, she realised that the two items that had been in there had gone.

With a loud shriek she ran downstairs to report the intruder to the lodging house Superintendant.

Chapter 7

'It's *so* good of you to let me occupy the building a week early,' Helen Trenchard enthused as Esther opened the front door to her with a big smile and stood back to let her in.

'Think nothing of it,' Esther assured her. 'I had nothing better to do and the property people told me that you want to do some building alterations. They also warned me not to let you make a start on them until you paid the first three month's rent in advance, but I won't tell them if you don't. Show me what you've got in mind, then I'll make us some tea. I hope you like gingerbread, because that's just about all I have left upstairs in the kitchen. In view of the early hour I imagine that you've not had any breakfast?'

'I never do, these days,' Helen replied, smiling, 'but I could certainly use a cup of tea after that horrible bus ride down from Hackney. Some people *never* wash these days, it would seem.'

'So what will you be doing to the place?' Esther enquired.

Helen pointed to the wide open and empty ground floor. 'I want to make this more like a proper set of office premises, with several rooms — including one for you, of course — so I'll need some dividing internal walls from floor to ceiling. Then we may need to subdivide that large storeroom up on the first floor, which from memory will involve replacing some of the fire-damaged panels that are still there.'

'I hope you weren't planning on doing all that yourself, with me helping you?'

'No, of course not.' Helen laughed pleasantly. 'I spoke to a Mr Bowden at Hemmingsworths and he promised to send some builder types down here this week to size up the job and give me a quote. Mainly joiners and painters, I'd imagine. Anyway, let's have that tea, then I can at long last put down this heavy bag, which contains most of my Alliance documents. One of them is my provisional idea of how the offices will eventually look.'

'Tell me more about your organisation,' Esther invited Helen as they sat across from each other in the kitchen, spreading the last of Esther's butter on the remains of her slightly stale gingerbread. Helen gazed sightlessly at the far wall as she began.

'It's called "The National Women's Labour Alliance" and in the fullness of time I hope that it will represent all working-class women throughout the nation. It's about time somebody did.'

'Represent them in what, exactly?'

'Parliament, newspaper columns, negotiations with individual employers and their organisations — everything. Women are so undervalued and underrepresented in both public life and control of their working conditions.'

'I certainly know all about the undervalued part.' Esther grimaced, remembering her recent encounter with the patronising vicar who'd be marrying her to Jack. 'And I can only assume that you've had similar experiences, else you wouldn't be taking on such an ambitious project.'

'All my life,' Helen confirmed. 'I was brought up in Blandford, in Dorset, where my parents ran a drapery store in the main street. That was how I developed an interest in working conditions, but only for men in those days. The countryside around us was largely given over to farming and heavily populated by labourers and their huge families, none of whom could afford to shop at our store. But their ragged children would congregate outside our premises, begging for any loose change that our customers might have left over, and when those customers complained my father would send me out to chase the beggars away. Gradually I began talking to them — and sometimes I gave them money out of my own allowance — and I soon learned about the terrible conditions they lived in, squatting in hovels with leaky roofs and no sanitation, scraping along on a few shillings a week, and so on.'

'But what's that got to do with working *women?*' Esther enquired, genuinely puzzled.

Helen smiled. 'Forgive me, I tend to get carried away. But during the course of associating with those field labourers, I became aware of the work of a woman who in those days was using her unique talents to assist in the formation of a trade union for agricultural labourers. You've heard of Annie Besant, I assume?'

'I can't say I have,' Esther admitted, 'but I rarely read the newspapers these days.'

'But you presumably heard about the Match Girls?'

'Of course,' Esther confirmed, 'that was difficult for even me to miss. Didn't they refuse to work until they got more money?'

'There was *much* more to it than that,' Helen enthused as she warmed to her theme. 'The conditions they were working under in that terrible factory down in Bow were little short of scandalous and the employers should have been prosecuted, except that there's no real criminal justice in this society of ours. The workers — mainly young girls — were exposed to something called phosphorous, which is one of the main ingredients of match heads. Well, continued exposure to that gave the girls something called "phossy jaw", which, as its name suggests, slowly rotted out their jawbones and in many cases led to death. As well as that, they were lucky to get five shillings a week for working with the permanent risk of death or disfigurement and their employers used all sorts of low tricks and excuses to "fine" them in order to pay them even less.'

'Disgraceful,' Esther muttered as she gestured with the tea pot. Helen nodded for more as she continued.

'What was even more disgraceful was that the business that employed them — "Bryant and May", it was called — proudly boasted to its shareholders two years ago that they'd made a massive profit of twenty-two per cent and that's when Annie Besant went into battle on behalf of the girls. She was working as a journalist in those days, although now I hear that she's joined some weird Eastern mystic cult or something. Anyway, she published a story about their plight and there was a massive rally and march through Regents Park, and several large parks in the East End, including Victoria Park, across the road from where I've lived for many years now. That's where I finally met up with Annie herself and a friend of hers and fellow organiser, called Clementina Black. I hope all these names aren't just flying over the top of your head, because they're important.'

'Not at all,' Esther assured her, fascinated by the recent history of her own community that she was learning for the first time. 'I remember all the fuss about the marches and rallies — that was only two years or so ago, wasn't it? I remember because it was just before I met my fiancé, when all those dreadful killings started down the road here, in Whitechapel and Spitalfields.'

'That's right,' Helen confirmed, 'and it was partly the public fascination with those that tended to take the issue of the Match Girls out of the public limelight. Anyway, to cut a long story short, Clementina and I began to meet and correspond, since we both had this long-standing interest in the rights of women at work, even though she was far better educated than me and was working as a teacher until she formed her own association.'

'So will she be working here with us?'

'Unfortunately not. Both Clementina and I remain committed to improving the position of women, but for her their working conditions have become part of a broader political campaign. She's become friendly with Eleanor Marx, who's the daughter of Karl Marx.'

'I've heard of him,' Esther announced proudly. 'He's the Socialist who's written a lot of books.'

'He died a few years ago, but yes, that was him. His daughter's kept up his work, it seems, and she and Clementina joined something called "The Women's Trade Union League". Then last year Clementina went out on her own with something else, called the "Women's Trade Union Association".'

'Forgive me for interrupting,' Esther said as she poured the last of the tea into her own cup, 'but with all these Associations that have sprung up recently, why is there still a need for yours?'

Helen smiled. 'A very intelligent — and very important — question, to which there's a straightforward answer. The likes of Annie Besant, Clementina Black and Eleanor Marx are very good at standing on platforms and preaching Socialism, "the Rights of the Working Man", and all that theoretical hot air, but in the meantime no-one's doing the obvious practical thing of actually organising the women into one national trade union that will provide a united front to the men in Parliament.'

'Aren't the men already doing that?' Esther enquired. 'I seem to recall that the dockers went on strike only last year and got themselves a minimum hourly wage. And didn't they cause a huge disturbance in Trafalgar Square on the same subject?'

'That was in connection with the Match Girls.' Helen frowned. 'Unfortunately the men in the trade union movement are primarily only out for their own interests and one of those, regrettably, is the opportunity for a good fight with police officers. Have you heard of somewhere called "The Fenian Barracks"?'

'No,' Esther admitted, 'but I know all about gangs of working men using any and every excuse to batter policemen. My fiancé's one of them.'

'He might want to consider another career,' Helen muttered.

'That's what his mother's always telling him, but what about this "Barracks" place? It sounds like an army camp.'

'It's the next best thing, except that the army in question consists of Irish troublemakers who'll leap onto any cause for the excuse to cause a disturbance and challenge the English authorities. It's a block of streets in Poplar, where all the residents have Irish names and a "no co-operation" attitude towards the authorities in general. Quite a few of the Match Girls lived down that way — do I need to explain further?'

'So the Trafalgar Square riots had basically nothing to do with supporting the Match Girls?'

'No, not really. As usual, hypocrisy won the day and a pretended support for working-class women and girls was just a front for a different political agenda. And of course the men hate us forming our own unions, simply because we're women. We're reaping the harvest sown by those other crusading women who think that they're entitled to the vote and a seat in Parliament.'

'But surely you agree with that as well?' Esther argued, now thoroughly confused.

'Of course, but not as a first priority,' Helen replied. 'For as long as women are seen as the lowest of the low, in the most humiliating and meaningless jobs, paid pittances for fourteen hour days and generally used and misused, they'll never be taken seriously by the politicians. So, step one is to get them equal status and equal pay and even that's been undermined by the men.'

'In what way?'

Helen allowed herself a bitter snort before she explained. 'Two years ago, my misguided friend Clementina Black was one of only two women who were allowed to attend as delegates to the male dominated Trades Union Congress. She was condescendingly allowed to put forward a motion for equal pay for women and was still congratulating herself on this barrier-breaking achievement when the male delegates agreed to vote for it only because the existence of lower pay rates for women threatened male jobs. Put crudely, if an employer can get a woman to do a job for five shillings a week, why would he employ a man to do the same job for ten shillings?'

'From what you've been telling me,' Esther observed thoughtfully, 'I'm surprised that the men's unions are prepared to tolerate women's unions in their midst.'

'Some of them aren't, believe me.' Helen laughed ironically. 'But up to now there's been no strong opposition because there's never been a powerful and united women's union movement. For as long as the men can boast of large unions full of strapping healthy men in industries such as the docks, the coal mines and the shipyards, they can present quite a physical presence, leaving aside the fact that the withdrawal of their labour in, say, the docks, can have such dire consequences for commercial interests in the city. How much threat do you imagine is posed by a "National Association of Bookbinders", or the "British Society of Upholsteresses"?'

Esther giggled. 'That was a joke, I take it?'

'Regrettably not. Both of those unions exist. But they exist in isolation. If they were merely a component part of a massive organisation consisting of every woman currently working in British industry and commerce, would they not be listened to more seriously? My sisters in female unionism have so far missed that point entirely. They've encouraged all these industry-based women's unions to develop in isolation and their political potential was well illustrated by your giggle a moment ago.'

'So you're going to bring all these unions together?'

Helen shook her head. 'Not the unions, no. What I'm setting out to do is to form one single enormous union with perhaps a hundred thousand members, all of them women working in traditional female industries — clothing manufacture, hotel and catering, food processing and so on — who can speak for all working women everywhere. Even street prostitutes, if necessary.'

'And how many have you got already?' Esther enquired, hoping that it didn't sound too much like a challenge.

Helen's eyes dropped to the table. 'Less than a thousand at present. Which reminds me...' She reached down into her copious carpet bag and extracted two large notebooks with hard covers, which she passed across the table to Esther. 'Your first job. This one is my attempt at a members' register. It currently has just over eight hundred names, but they need to be put in alphabetical order, so I've got you this new, and much larger, book, which as you can see is subdivided alphabetically. There are also a few more letters and suchlike stuck in amongst the pages, which are recent applications. You'll find references in there to money being enclosed with the letter, but I've extracted all those — mainly money orders — so you needn't worry on that score. But this other book here is where I've recorded all the payments, and I've opened a new Alliance bank account.'

'How much do the women pay to become members?'

'Fourpence a week, at present, as you'll soon see.'

Esther thought for a moment.

'Eight hundred members at fourpence a week will just about cover my weekly wage, but if you don't mind me asking, how are you going to support yourself and pay for these building alterations that you have in mind?'

'Obviously not from Alliance income at present. In due course I hope that the Alliance will become self-financing, but for the time being I'm eating into my own capital. I was left very comfortable as the result of a trust that my father set up for when he and Mother died and there's only my sister and myself who're beneficiaries. My sister's married to a doctor in Bristol, so she doesn't need the money and she's very graciously allowed me to take a greater share. But you can now understand why I might need to sell my house in Hackney.'

Just then they both became aware of someone hammering on the front door downstairs and Helen rose to her feet and took her diagram from the kitchen table.

'That's probably the building person come to give me a quote for the alterations. I'll go down and let him in, then once he's gone I'll go to that pie shop I saw when I got off the bus and get us something for dinner. And since you very unselfishly shared what looked like the last of your butter with me, I'll get some more of that as well.'

'While you're gone I'll make a start on this membership register.' Esther smiled back enthusiastically as she walked to the cupboard for her supply of pens and ink.

Chapter 8

Detective Sergeant Percy Enright sat across the desk from Chief Inspector Modley, wondering what was coming up next for him. He was thoroughly sick of investigating bank frauds, most of which seemed to be perpetrated by lowly clerical staff and he almost felt sorry for the last one he'd put away, who turned out to be a pimply young counter assistant with a weakness for horse race betting who'd been completely sucked in by a couple of sharks posing as a bookmaker and trainer, giving him the old 'we'll place your bets on certainties' routine. Percy much preferred the old-fashioned 'blood and guts' enquiries.

'We're pulling you out of Frauds, Sergeant,' Modley advised him as he lifted a small file from the desk in front of him and waved it from side to side like a fan. 'We've got a job for you "up West" that requires a fresh set of eyes and an unbiased viewpoint. I take it that you'll now be free to work on it?'

Percy frowned slightly as he saw his free days melting away before his eyes.

'I'm due in court on that Pimlico murder shortly, sir,' he reminded Modley, 'and since I hear that Bradley's being represented by Marshall Hall, I thought I'd spend some time refreshing my memory on some of the finer points of detail.'

'Do that in your own time, Sergeant. This one can't wait, because I need to know if it's linked in some way to a much wider investigation that we've been conducting for some time. You may have heard something about it in the tea-room — "the hotel wars"?'

'Only vaguely, sir.'

'Well, prepare to become better informed. There are two hotel and restaurant companies in the West End that are in bitter competition with each other. "Bitter" in the sense of setting fire to each other's premises, threatening each other's staff as they enter and leave their places of employment, pasting derogatory posters about each other on walls, and so on. I'm sure you get the picture. Anyway, one of the women employed as a waitress in the "Welbeck Rooms" owned by one of the companies was attacked in her flat two evenings ago when she returned home late at night after work. It may be the work of some random sexual maniac, or it may be another round of "hate" activities by her employer's rival. That's for you to find out and we need fresh eyes on this because I don't want the existing team drawing the wrong conclusions and muddying the waters in the main enquiry. You with me?'

'Fully, sir. I assume that the necessary details are in that folder in your hand?'

'No,' Modley replied in one of his habitual attempts at sarcastic humour, 'I was swatting flies. Here, take the file and report back directly to me. The woman should be at home, since her employers gave her a few days' paid holiday while she gets over the shock of it all. Go gently with her.'

Two hours later, after leaving his best suit at a dry cleaners at the insistence of his wife Beattie, who had calculated that if she nagged him for long enough it might be ready by the date of the wedding, Percy was admitted to the flat in Holborn by a frightened looking girl in her early twenties, who looked fearfully out into the corridor before slamming the door behind them and fastening the internal bolt. She waved Percy into the only chair and sat on the edge of the single bed, wringing her hands nervously.

Percy took a quick look around. It was a typical single room of the type converted from former grander buildings, probably once dedicated to insurance and then rented out on a weekly basis by one of those property development companies that seemed to be springing up everywhere. The room contained a bed and a table and chair, with a wash-stand and gas ring in the corner. Anything grander than that, and certainly any dish-washing, must be conducted in the communal kitchen that Percy had spotted on the ground floor on his way in. There were a few plain black dresses hanging on hooks from the wall and some sort of basket that presumably contained all Miss Beckwith's remaining clothing.

Percy introduced himself and showed the girl his police badge, provoking the usual response.

'I told everything I could remember ter that other bobby what come round the night it 'appened,' the girl assured him, 'an' why ain't yer in uniform, like 'e was?'

'I'm a detective from Scotland Yard, Miss Beckwith,' Percy explained.

'Is that more important than them uniformed bobbies? Whaddyer expect me ter tell yer other than what I told that uvver one?'

Percy was used to that reaction and gave the girl the standard explanation.

'We find that often a witness will remember some additional important detail that they'd overlooked when giving their first statement, Miss.'

'Call me Lillian. I'm 'ardly likely ter 'ave forgot owt, am I? It's not every day yer gets attacked by a maniac.'

'If you could just take me through it again, as you remember it, Lillian,' Percy said gently. He noticed her hands begin to shake as she closed her eyes and went back through it all.

'Well, I'd just got 'ome from work — I do waitressin' up at the Welbeck Rooms in Denmark Street — an' I were on what we calls "late turn" this week. It musta bin around midnight when I opened that door wi' me only key an' walked in, intendin' ter go straight ter bed, 'cos I were that worn out. The geezer what done me musta bin 'idin' be'ind the door, 'cos I'd just noticed as 'ow that basket in the corner were on it's side, wi' all me clothes all over the floor, when I were grabbed from be'ind. It were definitely a bloke, 'cos 'e were that strong an' 'e spoke ter me. Then the bastard 'eld me round the neck wi' one 'and an' started feelin' me up wi' the other. I were shoutin' the odds, but then 'e put 'is 'and over me mouth an' wi' 'is other 'and 'e — well, 'e ...'

She seemed to freeze at that point, then uttered a cry like a wounded animal and grabbed the cloth from beside her on the bed and broke into pitiful sobs. Percy was used to this sort of emotion from victims of sexual assault and let her tears run freely while he sat patiently with his notebook and pencil, wishing that the Yard had female officers to whom jobs like this could be assigned. There was nothing the girl had said yet that wasn't already in the file on his knee, and he could wait. Eventually she regained her self-control and apologised for her outburst.

'That's quite alright, Lillian,' Percy reassured her. 'Every girl who's ever been through that sort of experience reacts in the same way. I've spoken to dozens like you in the past and if it helps you explain what happened next, let me tell you that I'm a married man and have been for over twenty years, and I don't embarrass easily.'

'The bastard ripped me underwear off!' Lillian blurted out without further prompting.

'Anything else?' Percy enquired encouragingly.

'Ain't that enough? Dirty rotten bastard made off wi' me second best knickers. White, they was.'

'Have you any idea why he didn't attack you further?' Percy enquired.

Lillian shook her head.

'Maybe 'e just wanted me knickers, dirty bastard. Or maybe it were because o' the noise I were makin'.'

'You were screaming?'

'Damn *right* I were screamin'! Sorry about that — but what would *you* 'ave done in the circumstances?'

'Quite. But then he made off, carrying your — your undergarments?'

'Yeah, 'e legged it down the stairs an' I just collapsed on me bed 'ere an' bust out cryin' an' yellin'. Mr an' Mrs Adams from across the landin' come in, then called the police.'

'Do you happen to know if anyone saw the man leaving?' Percy enquired hopefully.

Lillian shook her head. 'That other bobby asked the same thing, but everyone else were asleep until they 'eard the commotion o' the police arrivin'.'

'According to the original police report, there was no indication that your door had been forced,' Percy reminded her. 'Are you sure you left it locked when you went out earlier in the day?'

'*Course* I'm sure,' Lillian insisted defiantly. 'A girl can't be too careful these days, what wi' all them murders. Mind you, fat lot o' use *that* were, as it turned out.'

'You said that the man said something to you,' Percy reminded her. 'Can you recall what it was, exactly?'

Lillian shrugged her shoulders.

'The other bobby never asked me about that. But it were summat stupid, like "Stay out o' the Union". I think 'e meant the pub I sometimes goes to, down the bottom o' Chancery Lane there. I won't be goin' back *there* again, let me tell you.'

'Anything else you can remember, that might help us to identify him?' Percy enquired hopefully.

'Only the smell.'

'The man had a distinctive body odour, you mean?'

'No, nowt like that. Not sweat nor nuffin'. More like 'e'd just washed 'is 'ands.'

'In your sink over there?'

'No, it were more like the stuff they make us use at work ter wash our 'ands — a strong sorta carbolic smell.'

Something else that wasn't on file, for all the use it might be, Percy concluded as he made his farewells and went back down through the common entrance and out into the side alley. He was reminded of the days he'd spent working on the 'Ripper' enquiry, a series of murders made that much easier by the prevalence of alleys such as this one, where men could easily lurk after dark. Men with sexual agendas. Men who preyed on innocent girls like Lillian Beckwith. Dirty rotten reptiles that he'd like to line up against a wall and take his billy club to.

Then he reminded himself that *he* was also a man, but that he was also a police officer. It was up to the likes of him to put a stop to what Lillian and other all-too vulnerable females were exposed to.

Chapter 9

'Why would I pay fifty pounds for a wedding dress when I could buy a simple white dress and add all those trimmings myself?' Esther demanded as she and Jack stood sheltering from the sleet flurries in the doorway of yet another department store in Regent Street that was closed because it was Sunday.

'You're surely not serious?' Jack demanded, appalled at the suggestion, but not entirely convinced that Esther wasn't capable of carrying it off.

'Of course I'm serious,' Esther insisted, 'I'm a seamstress, remember.'

'Used to be,' Jack reminded her.

'All right, *used* to be,' Esther conceded, 'but that's not a set of skills you lose easily. These dresses in the window, and for that matter the previous four windows we looked in, are a complete swindle. You take a basic fabric like cotton, or even silk, and you add a bit of lace and hand embroidery, stick a few pressed flowers on the finished product and charge five times the original cost of the material. Queen Victoria has a lot to answer for, getting all tarted up in that long thing that looked as if a curtain had fallen on her during her walk into the Chapel Royal. Isaac used to have a photograph of her on her wedding day pinned to the kitchen wall where we had to look at it every day and it's a wonder she could even stand upright in all that heavy frippery.'

'*Please* don't say things like that in front of Mother,' Jack pleaded. 'This wedding means so much to her.'

'I'd rather hoped it meant something to *us* too,' Esther replied starchily. 'But all I'm saying is that I could make my own wedding dress and no-one, not even a designer, would know the difference.'

'Have you ever made a wedding dress in the past?' Jack queried.

'No, but only because no-one asked. We were in bespoke daywear mainly, but bear in mind that my parents were fabric importers and I know how cheap the basic material can be. It's the dressmakers who put on all the additional frills that add so much to the price of the final garment — like these in the window.'

Jack sighed. 'I can see that you're wearing your determined face and I don't want to ruin the day by arguing with you. You looked so happy when I first called round to pick you up.'

'That had a lot to do with the fact that I had you all to myself for an entire Sunday, without having to travel to Barking for one of your mother's compulsory Sunday dinners. Even Uncle Percy seems to have got out of attending and I can only once remember seeing your Aunt Beattie there. How did she manage to earn her release?'

'It's a long story and has a lot to do with Aunt Beattie's support for my joining the police service. When Mother tried to get her on her side to talk me out of it, Aunt Beattie told her that it was what Uncle Percy had set his heart on and that she owed her first loyalty to her husband. There's been a certain coolness between them ever since and Uncle Percy only keeps turning up these days because Betty's such a good cook, whereas Aunt Beattie tends to cremate everything. Believe me, you wouldn't want to take cooking lessons from her.'

'And I don't need to take dress-making lessons from *anyone*, so here's what I suggest. I make my own wedding dress in secret, for less than ten pounds, then let's see if anyone can tell that it didn't come from up the West End.'

'If you say so, but there'll be Hell to pay if you ever lose patience when Mother's in one of her domineering moods — which is most of the time — and throw up in her face that you fooled her with your wedding dress.'

'I promise I won't, but you just reminded me — when do we have to see that awful vicar again?'

'We have to make another appointment. Let's make it for a Saturday, have supper with Mother the same day and then we'll have another Sunday free to look at houses.'

'If we must, but don't expect me to remain civil if that drip-nosed idiot starts lecturing me all about marriage.'

The next day, Esther finally found herself coming to the end of the painstaking task of compiling an alphabetical list of Alliance members. She'd opted to do it the hard way, rather than make mistakes in the impressive looking register that Helen had supplied her with, so had begun by copying, onto a separate list, all the names and addresses from the original book that Helen had begun, which was something of a disorganised mess and had convinced Esther that Helen did indeed need someone with her talents behind her. Then she'd taken the long list and under-scored the surnames in such a way as to make the first letter more prominent. The final stage had then been to copy them into the 'fair' book, as she called it.

She'd got as far as halfway through the 'Ws' when the noise became almost unbearable. Bert Freeman and his workers from 'Eastside Joiners and Jobbers' had been walking up and down past Esther's desk in the centre of the open area on the ground floor with tape measures and pegs which they hammered into the floor. It had once been Isaac's desk and it was larger than the kitchen table, so that made two good reasons why Esther preferred to use it for this important opening task in her new role as Helen's assistant. But the desk seemed to be smack bang in the middle of the centre line down which Bert and his men intended to erect the panelling that would separate the intended outer office area from the meeting room and offices on the inside.

Having given the workmen their orders, Helen had — rather huffily, in Esther's opinion — kept well out of the way of the alterations, sitting upstairs in the kitchen to conduct her correspondence and open the day's incoming mail. She had left Esther in charge of answering any questions that the men might have and it had been a matter of pride to Esther that she hadn't once had to call Helen down into the main room, where she'd done her best to keep working.

Apart from the noise there were other irritations, not the least being the dreadful personal habits of Bert Freeman. Not content with singing, in a loud voice, the latest music hall ditties, some of which were a bit 'risqué', and yelling instructions to his men that could have been delivered at a normal voice level, he would from time to time stop, extract some sort of small silver box from his waistcoat pocket, take a pinch of whatever was inside it up his nose, then sneeze violently.

Esther was familiar enough with the disgusting habit of snuff-taking, but she had never been exposed to it in such an enclosed space for such a lengthy period of time and the smell of it tended to give her a headache if she got too close to it. As a consequence, she had diplomatically left the front door open, but that then allowed in the noise of the carriages clattering up and down Lamb Street. Ordinarily she would have complained about the smell of horse dung that occasionally wafted in as well, but it was somehow preferable to Bert's snuff.

'I'm afraid yer'll need ter move that desk, Miss,' Bert advised her as he talked to her bosom as usual. 'We need ter come straight through where yer sittin'.'

Esther had been expecting this, so wasn't entirely surprised, but it was annoying, with the register almost completed.

'Very well, I'll go for a walk. How long will you be?'

'The rest o' the day, I'm afraid, and maybe tomorrer an' all. Don't worry, we'll move yer desk for yer an' put it back inside the little room we're makin' fer yer. It'll be nice an' cosy in there when we're done, but enough room fer a friend an' all, if yer get me meanin'.'

Not sure that she wanted to get his meaning, Esther left her desk as it was and walked upstairs for her handbag. She popped her head round the kitchen door to where Helen appeared to be frowning over a heap of correspondence on her desk.

'The workmen need me to move out of where I was working,' Esther announced, 'so if it's alright with you, I'll just nip down Commercial Street and do some shopping.'

'Yes, of course,' Helen agreed. 'I really need to carry on working on all these letters, so tell the foreman that if they want anything I'll be up here. And if you're going down Commercial Street, could you call in at the printing and stationery shop and ask them to print off another ream of Alliance letter paper?'

Esther gave the requested instruction to Bert Freeman, then set off with a light heart and a determined stride towards the drapery shops whose windows she'd often gazed into during her poorer days, when she had dreamed of buying a length of material and making her own wedding dress. She'd always regarded it as some sort of fairy-tale, but now that she was what Jack chose to call an 'heiress', the dream had become a reality.

When she returned almost two hours later, with a roll of white cotton and a dress pattern, the building was empty. Helen had left a brief note on the kitchen table, Esther's desk was over in a corner on the ground floor, and all the workmen had left. She could either spend the evening at the kitchen table, cutting out the dress from the pattern, or she could finish the members' register.

But the decision was taken out of her hands when she discovered that her provisional members' list was missing from the table.

Chapter 10

'It was a very unpleasant attack and definitely one of a sexual nature,' Percy advised Chief Inspector Modley the following morning, 'but I couldn't really say that it was linked in any way to the business rivalry between her employer and the other hotel company.'

'What sort of sexual nature?'

'Indecent assault and removal of an undergarment that the assailant took away with him. What you might call a specialised sort of offence. I've come across that sort before, although usually they steal from washing lines.'

The Chief Inspector sat back in his chair and thought for a few moments before responding, which he did with a disapproving frown.

'All the same, we need to ensure that the women of this city are protected from that sort of behaviour. And, as you say, it seems to bear the hallmark of a petty pervert. But current thinking is that pathetic idiots like that can often become emboldened into doing worse, so perhaps you'd better liaise with our colleagues in Burglary and see if they can match it with other reports of a like nature. Best to nip this in the bud before it escalates.'

'Why not the Sex Crimes Division, sir? Surely it's more in their line of work.'

'Partly because I'm telling you and partly because Burglary seem to have a promising new technique for solving their caseload. I was at a quarterly meeting for senior officers only a couple of weeks ago, when Chief Superintendent Morton was explaining how the officers under his command now regularly exchange case files and talk among themselves. It's not long before similarities appear in techniques — methods of entry, items stolen and so on — so that one man can be detailed to investigate more fully a series of break-ins that seem to have a common link. Apparently burglars and suchlike work to a definite pattern and all but leave their calling card at the scene of the crime. There was one bloke, for example, who always stole cheap cameo brooches, leaving behind far more valuable items. When some undercover men went down to the Sunday Market in Petticoat Lane, they found their man flogging them from a stall and had him buckled before the majority of the prospective purchasers had arrived.'

'So you think our man may be selling second-hand underwear from a market stall somewhere?' Percy enquired.

The Chief Inspector snorted. 'I'll assume that was intended as a joke and not a totally asinine suggestion. What I'm instructing you to do is go down the hallway to Burglary and see if they've got anything similar.'

'Anyone in particular in Burglary that I should speak to, sir?'

'Yes — anyone who can supply you with details of similar incidents. Use your initiative and get on with it.'

Jack sat at the long desk in the Burglary end of the Second Floor, trying to cheer himself up by listening to the distant sound of the Christmas Carol singers who were collecting for charity among the shoppers in Whitehall immediately below the long window at the end of the room. He was reminded that he and Esther had agreed to meet for a midday meal ahead of going shopping for Christmas presents and that cheered him a little more, until he also remembered that his mother had insisted on them attending, not only for Christmas Day and

Boxing Day, which involved an overnight stay, but also the New Year celebrations that had in the past been known to drag on for days.

God alone knew that he needed cheering up after the depressing series of interviews that he'd spent three days conducting. Three days and three separate victims, although his immediate supervisor Inspector Grady had been correct in his provisional assessment that one man might be behind all three. But for all the additional information that Jack had been able to glean, that was about as close as they would ever be likely to get in the search for a very unpleasant sort of burglar.

First of all Annie Cudsworth, in her cramped Shoreditch third floor hovel, complaining bitterly about the loss of two items of underwear from her laundry basket while she'd been out at work. The additional warning written on her wall was a puzzle and somehow took any possible humour out of the matter. The paper had printed, in the very centre and in large capital letters, the message 'Don't join up' and when Jack had asked her what she took the message to mean, she wasn't able to help beyond a vague suggestion that she'd been asked by someone to get colleagues in her workplace to group together and pay fourpence a week towards some sort of Friendly Society.

Then there was Clarrie Posnett, a fish gutter from Wapping, who'd also come home late that same afternoon to the sight of all her underwear in a pile on her bed, with a letter lying on her pillow with the same typewritten message: 'Don't join up'. Again, the victim was unable to supply any real clue as to what it might mean, other than the fact that someone at her place of work had received a letter inviting them all to meet together one evening in a local park to discuss the possibility of seeking a higher price per pound for the gutting work they did.

Finally, and perhaps the most chilling of all, Martha Pinkney, who'd awoken from sleep in her room in a Golders Green lodging house to see the vague outline of a man rifling through her clothing drawer and throwing items silently around the room. Her canary had been squawking out a warning from its cage in the corner and Martha had barely managed to suppress a scream as she lay there fearfully in her bed while the man walked towards the cage. But instead of reaching in and strangling the bird, as Martha had feared, he'd simply stuck a piece of paper to the cage and when Martha finally summoned up the courage to slip out from under the covers, she'd retrieved the note and called the police. The note read 'Don't join if you want to live'. Nothing had been stolen, but Martha was only able to advise Jack that a week previously she'd been visited by some woman who wanted her to organise her fellow employees in the metal works where she was a machine hand into some sort of organisation.

Jack sighed heavily and tried to apply his recent training to the task of identifying and listing the obvious common factors. All women. All single. All living in humble accommodation. Always an almost meaningless note and an interest in women's undergarments. And, in every case, a report of a strong chemical sort of smell, although each victim described it in different ways — peppermint, carbolic soap and smelling salts. No sign of any break in, which was unusual, given that these doss house doors normally yielded to a sharp kick, as had been demonstrated on many of the raids to which Jack had been a mere observer until the door was in. Then again, he reasoned, cracking even a rotting wooden door frame in a crowded rooming house was bound to create a noise and bring observers to their doors on the cramped landings. And in any case, whoever this offender was — and Jack was all but convinced that it was the same one, and a man — they clearly had a more subtle way of gaining entry.

Down the hallway, the desk sergeant was dealing with two people at once, although they seemed to know each other.

'Hello Uncle Percy!' Esther enthused as she leaned forward and gave him a peck on the cheek. 'Are you here to join Jack and myself for a meat pie, before we go Christmas shopping?'

'No, just dropping this file off, then I'm going home to rehearse for a trial that starts tomorrow. Hopefully it'll be over by Christmas, when we all have to celebrate not only the birth of Christ, but also the recent triumphs at bridge of your future mother-in-law.'

Esther giggled and wagged her finger admonishingly at him.

'I'll tell her you said that, then you'll wish you'd never accepted her invitation.'

'I had no choice,' Percy grimaced. 'Beattie accepted for both of us, but at least we'll be doing humanity a favour by not allowing my good lady to set fire to yet another turkey. My gastric system may even survive until the New Year, when I'm advised that we have to return to do it all over again.'

'Have you got much in the way of holidays due to you?' Esther enquired.

'Just the three public holidays, but I've put in for January 2nd as well, in the happy expectation that my hangover will last until then.'

'Jack's got an entire week and we're hoping to start looking for houses.'

'This is all very fascinating,' the desk sergeant observed from behind his half-open window, 'but do you think you could take your family reunion somewhere else? Was there something you wanted, Sergeant, or was this just a convenient place to put this file down?'

'Yes, sorry, the file's for you lot. Would you see that this gets to the right person, please?'

The desk sergeant took another look at the name of the officer in charge of the file.

'Enright. You related to Jack Enright?'

'I'm his uncle.'

'He's in the room down the end of the hall there, if you'd like me to go and get him.'

'No thank you,' Percy replied. 'I'll get to see quite enough of him over Christmas and the New Year. But this beautiful young lady's his fiancée and I'm reliably informed that she wants to take him out for dinner.'

Later that afternoon, Esther and Helen were sitting together in the kitchen going through Alliance correspondence. Helen tutted loudly as she read the letter she had just opened and took a mouthful of the tea that Esther had poured into her cup. Then she grimaced and put the cup down.

'Forgot the tea and sugar, sorry. But I was distracted by this. It's the third resignation from the Alliance this week.'

'But we did get six more members last week,' Esther reminded her.

'Yes, but this one was important,' Helen replied. 'Lillian Beckwith, from Holborn. Apart from the fact that we have very few members from the wealthier parts of town, I had high hopes for this one. She works for a hotel group and as you probably know there are a high proportion of women working in the catering trades. They aren't of any interest to the men's unions, so they're a potential source of a considerable number of members for the Alliance. I went to the trouble of meeting with over twenty of them when they left work one afternoon and Lillian was so enthusiastic that she offered to organise the others for me and collect their membership subscriptions every week. Now it seems that she's changed her mind.'

'Did she give any reason?' Esther enquired.

'None that makes any sense. She claims to have been attacked by a man in her room who warned her off joining a union.'

'Was she badly injured?'

'More shocked than anything, I'd imagine. Apparently the man took off with her undergarments.'

'I beg your pardon?' Esther was not sure whether to laugh or not.

'Apparently he stole her underwear. The things she was wearing at the time, according to this letter.'

'How horrible!' Esther exclaimed as she put down her toast.

'Anyway, it was horrible enough for her to ask that her membership application be removed from the file and that she be excused from paying any more membership dues, or collecting them from her fellow workers.'

'That's understandable, I suppose,' Esther thought out loud, 'after a dreadful experience like that. But she's sure that the threat that led to her resignation is connected with the theft of her — her underwear?'

'Quite sure, in her own mind. But then something like that can lead to severe shock and perhaps she confused the two. I'll have to take a trip up there and speak to her more closely, but I can well understand how horrible it must have been. Something like that happened to me the day before I first met you. That had to do with my underwear and there was a note telling me that only I could stop it happening again, although it didn't specify how.'

Her hand had begun to tremble and she put down the cup. Esther reached out and placed her hand over hers.

'Would you like to talk about it?'

'Definitely not. Let's keep this businesslike, shall we? This resignation will have to be recorded. Did you record the others?'

'Yes, of course, although it made the relevant register pages look a bit messy. Actually, I was going to speak to you about that. While I was in the stationers' shop the other day I was looking at a new sort of filing system. At least, it's one that I've never seen before. It's very simple, but very effective — just a series of cards that you keep in a box. You place each entry on a separate card, then you file them in the box in alphabetical order. It means that we can add to them as we go along, then when something like today's resignation comes along, we simply remove the card. The starting box and cards cost just under a pound, but then you can buy more packets of cards as you need them, for less than two shillings a packet. We'll need more than one box, obviously, but what do you think?'

'Just go ahead and do it,' Helen replied absently, her mind still preoccupied with something or other. 'Have you completed the original membership register yet?'

'Almost. I'd nearly finished when the workmen needed me to move my desk to make way for the room divider. Then the rough draft of the membership list that I'd painstakingly drawn up went missing for a day or so, but I found it lying on the floor after the men had finished their work. It must have fallen off my desk when they moved it.'

'They *have* completely finished, haven't they?' Helen enquired, almost fearfully.

'As far as I know,' Esther assured her. 'It's been a lot quieter down there this week, anyway. And not so smelly, with no disrespect to Bert Freeman.'

'That smell,' Helen enquired with wide eyes and a slight quiver to her lips, 'did it remind you of anything?'

'If you mean the stink from that dreadful snuff that Bert was always sticking up his nose, it reminded me of the cough medicine that my mother would insist that I swallow when I took my usual winter colds when I was little. "Camphor", I believe it's called — why?'

'I'd rather not say,' Helen replied evasively with a slight shudder. 'But if it's still wafting around down there when you go downstairs, leave the front door open, would you?'

Chapter 11

Percy lit his pipe and inhaled the first lungful.

'I thought I might explode at one point in there. I believe that four mince pies comes close to being a mortal sin. I hope they served Samuel Bradley bread and water for his Christmas lunch — that's all he deserves after getting off with Manslaughter. He poisoned his own wife, for God's sake!'

'I don't think Esther will want us to talk shop,' Jack replied as diplomatically as he could.

Esther snuggled up to him, kissed him on the cheek and smiled. 'As long as we're not in there listening to your mother droning on about her successes at bridge — card by card, no less — I don't care what we talk about.'

'In that case, young Jack,' Percy continued, greatly encouraged, 'and before your aunt comes to herd me back into her presence, did anyone pass on to you that file I left with your desk sergeant? He made the family connection and I rather imagine that it would have come to you first.'

'I haven't the faintest idea,' Jack replied. 'Mind you, it may well be somewhere in the pile of a dozen or so that got dumped on me just before I ran away for Christmas. They were all horrible and I decided not to ruin my little remaining "goodwill toward all men" by interviewing the victims. All vulnerable single women and all given horrible experiences by a slimy burglar.'

'Then you'll probably find mine somewhere in your pile,' Percy confirmed, 'since it involved exactly the same thing and I'm advised that you advanced types in Burglary now look for patterns in offending, rather than wearing out your boot leather pounding the pavement for real clues. Anyway, keep your eyes open for it. Name of Beckwith, from memory.'

'*Lillian* Beckwith?' Esther's ears pricked up at the name.

'I think so, why?' Percy enquired.

'From Holborn, or somewhere in that direction? Worked as a waitress and had a certain undergarment stolen from her person?'

'That certainly sounds like the one,' Percy agreed.

'Sounds like the cases I had just before Christmas,' Jack joined in with a grimace, 'since some of *my* victims lost them as well. But from their clothes drawers, not while they were wearing them. Anyway, it sounds as if your file belongs with mine.'

'How come you knew about this case?' Percy asked with one of his penetrating stares at Esther, just as Beattie emerged onto the lawn and called him back into the house.

'In a moment, my dear,' he called back. 'I'm just talking to Esther here. Get Constance to talk to the budgerigar if she's that desperate for an audience.' He turned back to Esther and lowered his voice. 'Esther, how did you know about this case?'

'It's connected with my new job and I seem to remember that the real objective of the attack was to dissuade the woman from joining the Alliance that my new employer is organising. It's a sort of female trade union.'

'The victim mentioned a union, right enough,' Percy confirmed, 'but she took it to mean her local pub.'

'Some of my victims were being warned off joining something as well!' Jack added. 'It certainly sounds as if all these cases are connected. I'll have a read of your file first thing when I get back to work.'

'You've got a week's house-hunting before that,' Esther reminded him. 'But I think your first job will need to be to come down to where I work and talk to Helen, because from what I could gather she was another victim and I don't think she ever reported anything.'

'Percy — *now*!' Beattie shouted from where she was standing, hands on hips, by the washing line.

'Coming, dear,' Percy replied, before turning back to Esther with a grin. 'Now there's a woman who *definitely* doesn't need a union in order to get her point across.'

Chapter 12

Jack turned the key in the front door lock and pushed the door open. The smell of dust that met them was not promising, but the set of rooms was exactly what they had in mind, the purchase price suggested by the property company was within their budget and Clerkenwell was respectable enough even for Constance Enright not to completely disapprove.

'It's been empty for several months,' Jack reminded Esther as they stood shivering in the hallway. Outside it was snowing heavily and they'd been obliged to kick snow off their boots on the scraper at the front door before entering by way of the front hall, and by the time they'd reached the second floor they were almost dry, although they left a faint smear in the dust as they progressed down the inner hallway of the rooms they had come to inspect.

Esther pushed open the first door, then gave a muted squeal as something small and furry scuttled to the far corner of the room and sat there quivering.

'The rats are obviously still in residence,' she muttered as she eyeballed the creature and mentally defied it to come any closer.

'It's a mouse, not a rat,' Jack advised her with an amused grin.

'It's still living here, whatever it is,' Esther replied with a disgusted twist of her mouth. 'If we were to buy this place, do you know how to get rid of them?'

'Just put down some of Aunt Beattie's gravy,' he joked. 'That would poison anything.'

'Seriously, Jack — I *really* don't like rats.'

'Good job it's a mouse then,' he replied, still amused.

'Let's take a look at the other rooms,' Esther suggested frostily, 'and if they've got furry things in them as well, we'll go and look somewhere else.'

'This is the last on our list for today, remember,' Jack replied, 'and we didn't like the first three.'

'That place in Stepney was nice enough,' Esther reflected, 'and it had one more room than this place. But, as you tactfully pointed out, it's a bit too "East End" for your mother's liking.'

'We're the ones who have to live wherever we finish up,' Jack replied, 'and if we want to decorate it to our own tastes before the wedding, we'll need to find somewhere pretty soon.'

'We've already spent the first four days of your leave looking at places,' Esther replied glumly, 'so let's take a walk through this one, then you can take me for a late dinner somewhere.'

'Let's go and take a look at the view from the front window.'

'If we can see through all the muck and grime that's collected on it,' Esther observed unenthusiastically as she followed Jack to the window with one wary eye on the hole in the skirting board that the mouse had disappeared into. Through the window they could see down into the street and across it to another row of houses that seemed identical to the one they were inspecting. Carriages were passing back and forth and Jack pointed to a horse bus.

'The sign on the front of that says that it's heading for Holborn. From there I could change for Whitehall, so only two bus rides. And you could get down to Spitalfields on that Whitechapel service we saw as we walked up here.'

'Assuming I still have a job then,' Esther reminded him gloomily, 'which seems unlikely at the rate at which the Alliance is losing members.'

'Are they still leaving?' Jack replied.

Esther sighed and nodded. 'I was in there two days ago, while you were getting measured for your wedding suit and five more dropped out over Christmas. Poor old Helen's getting quite despondent.'

'I'm back to work next Monday,' Jack reminded her, 'so do you want me to call in then? We could have dinner together afterwards at that pie shop down the road from you.'

'Never let it be said that you don't know how to show a girl a good time,' Esther smiled as she leaned forward and kissed him on the lips. 'But yes, come down as soon as you're able. Now for the time being, let's have a look at the other rooms, which hopefully the mice will have left all to us.'

'It's going to need an awful lot of work,' Esther enthused over morning tea the following Monday, as she and Helen sat sorting through a week's correspondence, 'and there's a rather suspicious damp patch in the bathroom, but Jack reckons he can fix that, and the price was within our range, so it looks as if we'll shortly become the proud owners of a set of second floor rooms in Clerkenwell. The less fashionable half, unfortunately, but the suburb name should be enough to satisfy Jack's mother.'

'Is she a snob?' Helen enquired.

'Not so much a snob, but certainly very particular and of course she wants the best for her only son. What mother wouldn't?'

'And when will you be moving in?'

'Not until after the wedding, obviously and that's not until June, so we have plenty of time to decorate the place and get in things like carpets and so on. We've still got something left over from the money I got for this place and apparently Jack qualifies for part of the family trust fund when he gets married.

His younger sister got a payout of some sort when she got married last year and Jack's determined to get his share before his mother spends it all.'

'It must be a very exciting time for you,' Helen said, smiling, 'and I wish you all the best, even though I haven't met your fiancé yet.'

'He promised to come down here sometime in the next few days,' Esther advised her, 'and we think that there may be some pattern behind all these resignations you've been getting from the Alliance.'

'As you've probably already deduced,' Helen replied as her smile disappeared, 'I don't have a very high opinion of police officers, after my latest experience with them, but obviously I'm more than happy to meet your own young man, particularly since he seems to have made you a very happy person. Quite a treat to have around the place, in fact.'

'Did you never have a young man of your own, if you don't mind me asking?'

Helen nodded. 'I did, once upon a long time ago, but he died and since then, well to be perfectly frank with you, most of the men I meet in the union line of business are far too aggressive and domineering. Not my type at all.'

'So nobody since the one who died?' Esther probed.

Helen shook her head. 'There's one who'd still like to make what he would no doubt call an "honest woman" of me, but he's really not for me. He and I ought to be a good match, because he's also recently started up a union — woodworkers in his case — but he's not very engaging in personality, once you get below the surface of his somewhat greasy charm. You may have noticed the regular arrival of flowers here, for example.'

'I had noticed,' Esther replied diplomatically, 'but I didn't like to say anything, because of course it's none of my business. So they're from your gentleman admirer?'

'Yes, along with ridiculous sugary poems and suchlike that arrive almost weekly in the general mail. There's never any signature, as if I didn't recognise his over-ornate handwriting.'

'Nevertheless,' Esther persisted, 'a lot of women would be bowled over by romantic gestures like that.'

'I'm not a lot of women,' Helen insisted, 'and I've reached the somewhat mature age of thirty-five without some man in my life telling me how to lead it. So George Manners can go and drip his honeyed charm on someone who might appreciate it. Now, what's the net loss of membership this week, following all this post-Christmas correspondence?'

It was almost dinner time the following day before Esther was obliged to leave her desk inside the rather false looking 'office' that lay behind the dividing wall, walk through the hole in the panelling that might one day constitute a doorway and cross to the front door to answer the knock. Outside in the street stood an enthusiastic looking Jack, armed with what seemed to be a very heavy carpet bag, which he dumped onto the floor as soon as he had stepped inside and given Esther a warm kiss.

'Pie shop first,' he insisted. 'I'm fair famished. Tell your employer that a knight in shining armour commanded his horse to kick down the door and swept you off into the noonday sun for a banquet in his palace. Or at least a mutton pie at "Umberto's Trattoria", as it describes itself on the wall. That's Italian, isn't it? What happened to the Jewish cafes?'

'There never were any, so far as I can remember,' Esther replied, smiling. 'And take it from me that onion bialy is an acquired taste. Stay there for a moment while I nip upstairs and get my hat — it looks like more snow out there.'

An hour and a half later, Jack was shaking hands with Helen, somewhat formally, in the kitchen.

'As Esther may have told you, I don't really approve of policemen,' Helen warned him, 'but I'm prepared to suspend judgment in your case, since you've obviously made Esther so happy.'

'Can I get that in writing?' Jack said with a boyish grin. Helen became an instant convert as she smiled and offered Jack a seat while she put a pan on to boil for tea.

'I brought your bag upstairs, by the way,' she told Jack over her shoulder. 'I assumed that it has something to do with why you're here at Esther's insistence and doesn't just contain your laundry?'

Jack blushed slightly and nodded.

'No, it doesn't, but it has to do with laundry, I believe. Other people's, that is. Your members'?'

'That's about as helpful as my last conversation with a police officer,' Helen complained, but with a smile. 'Could you bring yourself to be a little more specific?'

'Sorry. The fact is that I work at Scotland Yard in something called the Burglary Division. As its name suggests, we look more carefully at reported break-ins to people's houses and rooms and look for patterns in them. I gather from talking to Esther that some of your members have recently received uninvited invasions of their homes during which certain items of clothing have been removed, or interfered with in some way. All of them have also received a warning against joining your union — the "Alliance", I believe it's called. And one in particular — a Miss Lillian Beckwith,' he added after a quick look inside his notebook. 'She seems to have suffered even more, according to the report that my uncle made.'

'Your *uncle*?' Helen queried.

Jack nodded. 'My Uncle Percy. He's a sergeant who works at the Yard, same as me. It was pure coincidence that his report landed in my pile and now I'm even more convinced that there's a pattern to all this.'

'You mean that all the poor unfortunate women who've been threatened into having nothing to do with the Alliance have suffered the same indignity?' Helen enquired.

'No, not all of them,' Jack explained. 'That's what makes all these incidents fall into a pattern. In my bag here are about a dozen or so reports from women who all received unpleasant visits — usually while they were out working — during which a piece of paper was left behind, warning them to refrain from joining a "union", as the notes call it. I'm prepared to work with the theory that the "union" in question is your Alliance.'

'These notes to which you're referring,' Helen asked, somewhat white in the face, 'were they typed on a single sheet of paper, with something else obscene written in pencil above it?'

'You've had one of these "visits" yourself, haven't you?' Esther said quietly as she reached out and placed her hand on Helen's trembling wrist.

Helen nodded. 'Yes, but I don't want to talk about it. Let's concentrate on what Jack has to tell us.'

'There's not really a lot more,' Jack admitted, 'except for the all-important "pattern" that I already mentioned.'

'You mean there's more?' Helen enquired. 'Surely the "pattern", as you call it, is in the fact that each note was warning away a potential member of the Alliance?'

'Yes and no,' Jack replied unhelpfully. 'Certainly they all have that in common, as I quickly spotted when I read the file reports. But some of them endured more than that, didn't they? Every one of them got the warning, but only some of them suffered the additional indignity regarding their underwear. It was only when Esther mentioned that Lillian Beckwith was an important link to what might have proved to be a fertile source of new members that it occurred to me that the "underwear" victims, if I may call them that, were singled out for special treatment by whoever carried out the break-ins. If it turns out that they — like Lillian Beckwith — were of additional importance to your Alliance, then we have our definite pattern. We also have a strong suggestion that whoever carried out these disgusting attacks was acting under orders from someone who understood the significance of the "special" ones and knew who to target more strongly and why. Someone very familiar with your recent recruitment drives.'

'I hope that doesn't make *me* a suspect?' Esther said, horror-stricken.

Helen reached out and placed a reassuring hand on her arm. 'Of course not, Esther. Apart from anything else, the break-in to my house occurred the day before I met you for the first time.'

'At the risk of having my engagement broken off, along with parts of my face,' Jack said, grinning, 'you have to accept that whoever's doing this will be someone you least suspect. Someone who knows your every move and may pose as a friend.'

'What about those other women you told me about?' Esther asked Helen. 'You know — the ones who formed unions of their own?'

'Out of the question,' Helen insisted. 'Apart from the fact that their moral principles would stand firmly in the way of such a thing, Annie's believed to be in India somewhere, whereas I read in the newspaper only yesterday that Clementina was in Manchester, addressing a group of women in the cotton trade.'

'Anyway,' Jack continued, 'what I'd like to do, if it's alright with you, is to compare the names of the victims in all these files I've brought with me with names from your membership lists. If they match up and if we can identify why some of them were important enough to merit "extra attention", shall we call it, in the matter of their undergarments, then we have a clear pattern we can work on.'

'We?' Helen enquired with raised eyebrows.

'Myself and Detective Sergeant Enright.'

'Your uncle?'

'The very same. He's hoping to be allowed to lead the enquiry, since it threatens to be a very wide-ranging business and whoever's been actually carrying out these break-ins, even though under orders from someone else, is clearly a very dangerous man.'

Percy was indeed hoping that he would be able to join Jack in what sounded like the sort of operation he liked — buckling bullies who enjoyed preying on people weaker than themselves. On the whole that meant men and he never failed to gain satisfaction of sorts from bringing in scum who thought that it was very big and brave to punch, kick and sexually abuse women. Percy liked it even more if these men resisted arrest and he could employ his billy club where it hurt the most.

But the look on Chief Inspector Modley's face suggested that Percy's next interview would be with yet another trembling bank clerk or pompous under-manager.

'I assume that this is a ruse designed to avoid going back to Fraud,' the Inspector scowled as he digested what Percy had just suggested. 'We have an entire department dedicated to keeping an eye on these union types, so why should I authorise you to run your own show on the side?'

'With all due respect to our colleagues in Unions,' Percy argued back, 'they're focused on male unions and the threat that they pose to law and order. The female unions, such as they are at present, are different and pose no such threat. And this isn't about unions per se anyway — it's about a disgusting slime bag who preys on vulnerable women.'

'Obviously I'm well aware of your role in nailing the Ripper,' Modley conceded, 'but from what you've managed to tell me so far, this man simply enjoys collecting ladies' underwear. Not quite the same thing as slashing throats in Whitechapel alleyways, is it?'

'It could develop into that,' Percy urged him. 'Men like that usually begin in a small — almost pathetic — way, for example stealing from clothes lines. Then after a while that isn't enough to give them the satisfaction they crave and they take to sneaking up on women, or peeping at them through open curtains. The next stage — like this one in Holborn — is some sort of sexual assault on the victim, which rapidly turns into rape, then finally — murder. It's a well documented pattern of offending and during our last conversation you were singing the praises of the team in Burglary, who have taken to studying patterns.'

'Like your nephew?'

'Yes, like him, certainly. But I'm not suggesting that we set up a family business. It just so happens that his current enquiries have revealed a pattern of sexualised criminal behaviour by a man who is at present merely a rather unpleasant burglar with a penchant for ladies' underwear, but who may develop into something far more ominous if we don't catch him now.'

'You're suggesting that you may have caught another Ripper in the formative years of his criminal career?'

'Yes, but also someone we need to take out of circulation because of the fear he's already instilling into innocent law-abiding women. His victims aren't street totties, sir — they're ordinary girls and slightly older women, still young enough to be attractive anyway, and they all do honest jobs. It's only a matter of time before word of this man's predatory behaviour leaks out to the newspapers, then it'll be a case of "Where was Scotland Yard?" and "What protection do we receive in return for the cost of our police force?". I want to nip this in the bud.'

Modley stared back at him, deep in thought as he played with the chain on the Albert watch tucked into his waistcoat pocket. Finally he nodded and Percy let out a long but subdued sigh of satisfaction.

'Very well, but no more than a month. If you haven't buckled your man by then, you're back to Fraud — understood?'

'Absolutely, and thank you, sir.'

Modley smiled. 'I don't like these creepy types any more than you do, Percy, but it's a question of maximising the effectiveness of our manpower.'

'I quite understand, sir and I think that the combined talents of the Enright contingent within the Yard will have this knocked on the head long before our month is out.'

Chapter 13

'This is my Uncle Percy,' Jack announced as he led him into the kitchen in which Helen and Esther sat waiting for them. 'He was the one who went to see Lillian Beckwith and got the full story from her. He doesn't bite, as Esther will confirm, but he's had twenty years more experience than me in catching bad people.'

'Delighted to make your acquaintance,' Helen said formally as she shook his hand, then removed it as soon as was polite to do so. 'Do sit down and have some tea.'

Percy thanked her, sat down and took out his notebook and pencil, before turning to Jack with a smile.

'Did Jack tell you what he and Esther discovered when they compared the burglary reports from the Yard files with your membership lists?' he enquired.

Helen nodded. 'Esther did. She tells me that every one of those who asked to cancel their membership had received one of those warning notes.'

'But some of them received more than that,' Jack reminded her. 'Every victim who suffered some sort of chilling interference with her underwear was someone whose continued membership was of particular importance to the Alliance, and in each case there was an additional note written in pencil, by some despicable type who's barely literate.'

'Like this, you mean?' Helen reached inside her handbag and produced the one she'd received. As Percy took it from her trembling hand and began to study it intently, she explained, 'It was stuck to the mirror of my dressing table and my first reaction was to throw it into the waste basket in my bedroom. Then when Esther told me about the note that Martha Pinkney got, I retrieved it. Fortunately I hadn't got round to emptying the basket, but the notes a bit crumpled I'm afraid.'

'That's not a problem,' Percy assured her as he gazed warmly into her green-blue eyes and took in the light ginger hair and freckled face that reminded him so much of a young Beattie. She caught the intensity of his gaze, blushed, and looked down at her lap as Percy broke his reverie and continued. 'We'll need to collect as many more of these as we can, if only to further confirm that we're dealing with the same man whose Board School education seems to have been a first class waste of public money.'

'I was planning on visiting some more of those who've cancelled their membership,' Esther chirped in, 'so I'll collect all the notes and bring them back here.'

'That should also help to separate the important ones from the others,' Jack observed to a faint snort from Helen.

'They're *all* important to me, young man, but I think what you meant was that we need to distinguish between the ones who could have brought in more members and those who couldn't.'

'Precisely,' Percy confirmed, 'and while you're at it, Esther, could you find out if each of the notes was affixed with the same sort of stuff as this, on the back of the note Helen received? I'd take a guess that it's some sort of putty — the sort that glaziers use for fixing glass into window frames. I believe plumbers use it as well, but at any rate it's something widely used in the building trades.'

'Do joiners use it?' Helen enquired in a wavering voice.

'Probably,' Percy replied, 'although obviously I'm not a joiner. Why do you ask?'

'How many of the other members who cancelled their subscriptions mentioned a strong smell in their rooms afterwards?'

'All the ones I interviewed,' Jack confirmed, 'but the smell seemed to be different in every case.'

'Lillian Beckwith described a smell of carbolic,' Percy added, then turned back to look Helen firmly in the eye. 'You smelt something as well, at a guess?'

'Yes indeed, but it was a sort of peppermint, although there was a hint of carbolic. It reminded me of when I was in hospital. But then, one day when the workmen were here, I smelt it again.'

'Bert Freeman!' Esther all but shouted. 'He was forever taking snuff and the smell of the stuff almost gassed me on occasions. But it wasn't always the same every day — are there different "flavours" of snuff, for want of a better word?'

'I wouldn't know,' Percy replied, 'since I smoke a pipe. But snuff is derived from tobacco and there are different "flavours", as Esther calls it, of tobacco, so why not snuff?'

Helen went pale and gripped the side of the kitchen table.

'To think that that dreadful man was in here for over a week! He broke into my bedroom drawer and had his hands in my ... my ...'

It all proved too much for her and she struggled vainly with the tears until she gave up the effort and laid her head on the table and sobbed. Esther moved quickly to her side and put her arms round her comfortingly, while indicating with a jerk of her head for Percy and Jack to make themselves scarce. They wandered outside into the rattle and rumble of passing vehicles, with the additional rhythmic clop of horses' hooves on the cobbles, as Percy lit his pipe and smiled.

'This is going to be easier than I feared, Jack my boy. All we need to do is collar this Bert Freeman character and "Bob's your uncle", as the popular saying goes. Except in this case, your uncle's Percy and we need an address for the firm that employed Freeman, and probably still does, unaware of his sideline in ladies' underthings.'

The front door opened and Esther slipped out to join them.

'I think she'll be alright, but perhaps it's best if we call it a day for now.'

'I think we've got all we need for the time being anyway.' Percy smiled. 'Except for dinner — whose treat is it?'

'Have you given any thought to where to go for your honeymoon?' Percy asked as they each sat hunched over something calling itself a 'ciabatta'. Percy had gone for what had once been ham, while for Esther the choice had been chicken and Jack had yet to work out what exactly was making his mouth burn and was hesitant to enquire further.

'Somewhere where they serve better rolls than this, I hope,' Esther commented.

Jack cleared his mouth and stared out at the passing traffic. 'I thought perhaps the South of France,' he mused out loud, 'or some moon-drenched beach in Tahiti. Or we could take a camel ride across the burning sands of Arabia, or go pearl diving in the glittering Pacific.'

'I had in mind Southend,' Percy replied with a smirk.

'*Southend*?' Jack and Esther shouted back in disbelieving unison, before Esther added, 'A week in Southend would be the end of our marriage before it had even begun!'

'I take it that was a joke, Uncle?' Jack said hopefully. 'Whereas Bournemouth, Brighton and suchlike are holiday resorts, Southend is more like a *last* resort!'

'Very funny,' Percy said, smiling, 'but humour me. An old school friend of your Aunt Beattie's now runs a guesthouse in Southend, right on the sea front and your aunt's been in my ear for the best part of a month now, campaigning for us to spend a weekend in the place. The only way I can shut her up is by suggesting that I talk you into spending your honeymoon there. If it's anything like our honeymoon in a holiday cottage in Suffolk, it won't matter what else there is to do, or even what the weather's like.'

'Uncle Percy!' Esther admonished him with a blush. 'I'm sure we'll find plenty of *other* things to do, so thank you but no thank you.'

'On the other hand...' Jack mused out loud with a lascivious grin, which disappeared when Esther punched him on the shoulder, relieving him of the obligation to burn his mouth further with whatever he had chosen for his dinner, as it flew out of his hand and landed on the narrow pavement beyond the door.

Jack looked out with a rueful smirk. 'Whatever that was, not even the sparrows seem to want it.'

'Leave the talking to me,' Percy instructed Jack later, as they prepared to enter the premises of 'Eastside Joiners and Jobbers' in Bow Road.

'Why?'

'Because I outrank you — twice,' Percy replied as he tapped the ash from his pipe onto the pavement with the aid of his boot heel. 'Once as your uncle and secondly as your sergeant.'

The bell above the front door tinkled faintly as they pushed it open and within a minute or so a man in a brown overall emerged from the back, a pencil stuck behind his ear and a notebook in his hand.

'What can I do fer you gents?' he enquired pleasantly, before his face froze as Percy produced his police badge from his inside pocket like a magician coaxing a rabbit from a top hat.

'We'd like to speak to a Mr Bert Freeman.'

'Never 'eard of 'im. Does 'e claim ter work 'ere?'

'Don't mess me about,' Percy warned him. 'Bert Freeman's your jobbing foreman.'

'No 'e's not,' the man replied confidently. 'That's 'Arry Broad'urst. Leastways, it were until 'e fell off a ladder a few weeks back. 'E won't be back on the job fer another fortnight, they reckon.'

'You recently carried out some work on premises in Lamb Street, Spitalfields?' Jack reminded him.

'Sounds familiar. Let me look at the order book. Let me see now, when were this exactly?'

'Mid to end of November,' Jack prompted him.

The man looked up with a smile.

'Yeah, 'ere it is, right enough. Internal dividin' walls an' a couple o' doors — that the one?'

'That's it,' Jack confirmed, and Percy added, 'And Bert Freeman was the foreman.'

'No 'e weren't,' the man insisted. 'The lads worked wi'out a foreman on that job. Yer got a complaint abou' the way it were done?'

'No,' Percy replied in a sharp voice that betrayed his mounting irritation, 'I just want to speak to Bert Freeman.'

'Well, like I said, yer can't,' the man insisted. 'I ain't never 'eard o' no Bert Freeman.'

Chapter 14

'One of the most valuable lessons I've learned during what I choose to call my illustrious police career,' Percy said to Jack as they stood, nonplussed, on the pavement outside Eastside Jobbers and Joiners, 'is never to accept the first answer you're given.'

'The bloke seemed pretty definite,' Jack observed.

'Particularly not the first answer you're given by someone who seems pretty definite,' Percy added. 'Did you notice his Adam's Apple?'

'Can't say I did,' Jack admitted.

'Always watch the Adam's Apple. His was going up and down faster than a tottie's skirts. A good sign of a bloke lying through his arse.'

'You reckon he knows Bert Freeman?'

'Not necessarily, but he knows that something wasn't quite right about that job in Lamb Street.'

'So where do we go now?'

'What time is it?'

Jack took his fob watch from his pocket. It had been left to him by his late father and it was his proudest possession. He flipped open the silver cover and examined the ornate numbering.

'A few minutes before five, why?'

Percy smiled and nodded across the road to 'The Volunteer's Arms'. 'In there,' he replied and began to stride away, forcing Jack to scurry after him.

'Why in here? Do you think Bert Freeman might be a patron?'

'No, but his workmates will be. It's across the road from where they sign off for the day and I'd bet Bermondsey to a brick that some of them will head straight in. We sit here and make a mental note of who goes in there to sign off, then we wait here until they cross the road for a light refreshment after their honest day's toil. Oh, ye of little faith,' Percy muttered as two workmen made their way from the front door of the joiners' office to the front door of the pub. 'Head for the Gents up the side alley, then we come back in as if we'd only just arrived. Follow me.'

Two minutes later the two workmen were barely into their first pint when they saw the police badge appear on the counter in front of them and turned to see Percy and Jack standing behind them.

'Sorry to disturb your well earned pints, my friends,' Percy purred politely, 'but I'm looking for a Mr Bert Freeman.'

'So am I, the arse'ole,' one of them replied as he spat into the sawdust. 'Borrered a quid off me on the Friday dinner time, then didn't bother showin' up fer work on the Monday. We 'ad ter finish the job ourselves, then report back ter Mr Jenston in the office.'

'Is he the bloke behind the counter in the shop across the road?' Percy enquired.

The man nodded.

'That's 'im, the pompous ol' shit. 'Im wi' the chrome dome an' the Newgate Knockers the colour o' rabbit shit.'

'Bald head and darkish side whiskers,' Percy explained to Jack by way of simultaneous translation. Then he turned back to his new found confidante. 'I take it that Mr Freeman wasn't your normal foreman?'

'No, that's 'Arry Broad'urst, but 'e took a turvey off a ladder an' busted 'is spanner.'

'Hand,' Percy translated for Jack's benefit, before turning back to the two men. 'So how were you advised that Mr Freeman was to become your foreman for the Lamb Street job?'

'We wasn't, not proper like,' the other man joined in. 'We turned up fer work on the previous Monday and was told ter report ter this office place in 'Oxton wi' the wagon. When we got there, it turned out ter be one o' them property offices an' the geezer in charge introduced us ter Bert Freeman an' told us that 'e were in charge o' the job we was assigned ter, an' ter foller 'is orders.'

'And you never saw Mr Freeman again, after that job?' Percy asked by way of confirmation.

Both men shook their heads.

'Like I said,' the first one repeated, 'we never even seen 'im again by the end o' *that* job an' we 'ad ter sign off on it ourselves.'

'Thank you very much, Mr —?'

'Timpson. John Timpson.'

'Now what?' Jack asked as they walked outside, where it had grown dark, but where a light was still shining from the window of the office across the road.

'Remember what I said, Jack? Never believe the first answer you're given? By the same token, never believe a name you're given so glibly by someone who has cause to be suspicious of police officers.'

'What do you mean?'

'That man we were speaking to — what name did he give?'

'Timpson.'

'Take a look back at the sign above the pub. What brand of beer do they sell?'

'Timpsons,' Jack repeated with a smile. 'But his story sounded credible.'

'So did Mr Jenston's,' Percy reminded him. 'Remember him? The one with the chrome dome? Time we went back in there and shook him warmly by the throat.'

Jenston looked up with a terrified expression as Percy kicked the door open in a dramatic gesture, slammed his police badge down on the shop counter and glared across at him.

'You're moments away from going down to the local cells on a charge of wasting police time, Mr Jenston. So don't waste any more of it — where will we find Mr Freeman?'

'I've no idea, 'onest! Never even met the man.'

'But you had sufficient confidence in his workmanship to leave him to supervise the work in Lamb Street?'

'That weren't my choice, honest it weren't. I wer just told ter direct the men ter 'Emmingsworth Properties in 'Oxton, where there were a new foreman waitin' ter supervise the job.'

'And who selected Mr Freeman for that job, exactly?'

'No idea — but it weren't the first time.'

'How do you mean?'

Jenston looked carefully round the office briefly, then lowered his voice.

'It's the union, yer understand? All the men are members an' the bloke what controls the union calls the shots regarding who we employ an' when. My boss, Mr Goldman, instructs me never to fall out wi' the union, else I'll be out of a job. An' occasionally we get a call from the union that so an' so will be allocated ter this job or the other an' no questions asked. So I don't.'

'And you got a call from the union to tell you that Mr Freeman would be supervising that job?'

'Not exactly in them terms, no. I got a telephone call — or rather, Mr Goldman did — from the union, to tell 'im to expect a call from 'Emmingsworth Properties about a job in Lamb Street, Spitalfields. Sure enough we did an' I took the call. It sounded too good to be true, since our normal foreman were off sick, like I told yer earlier, an' this job didn't need us ter supply one. I was to send the men up ter 'Emmingsworths, where they'd be getting a new foreman approved by them. An' that were it, honest.'

'If I find that you've left out anything important this time,' Percy said in a menacing tone, 'I'll be back here to stuff my fist down your throat and punch your arse out from the inside. Understood?'

Jenston nodded palely and Percy indicated with a jerk of his head in Jack's direction that it was time to take their leave.

As they stood outside on the pavement, Percy looked to Jack.

'May I take it that Hemmingsworth Properties was the lot that bought the building from Esther?'

'Yes, the name sounds familiar. Sounds as if they could tell us where Mr Freeman can be found.'

'They probably *could*, young Jack, but whether or not they *will* is a matter we can discover for ourselves tomorrow. It's all too convenient, don't you think? The joinery firm gets its orders from some sort of union and Helen Trenchard is trying to establish a women's trade union of sorts. I know enough about these new unions to appreciate that somebody somewhere may have a very good reason for doing very bad things. Not only do potential members of Helen's "Alliance", as I seem to remember it's called, get very unpleasant visits from a man who in some cases pays close attention to their underwear, but the alterations ordered by Helen were supervised by a man supplied by her landlords. A man, what's more, who was seemingly planted in there by a rival union. Not only that, but if we believe the noses of some of the victims then the same man who posed as a joinery foreman was also given the task of frightening off potential members of the Alliance.'

'And we're no nearer to finding out his real identity,' Jack observed glumly.

'Perhaps *we* aren't, but there are certain new leads we can follow up.'

'Such as?'

'And here was I fondly imagining that my nephew had turned into a detective. Number One — could you have supervised the alterations inside the Alliance office?'

'Of course not — I'm not a joiner.'

'There you are, then — lead Number One. At some stage in his miserable life, our Mr Freeman was trained as a joiner. Number Two — he's addicted to taking snuff.'

'And Number Three?'

'He probably already has a criminal record.'

'But not as "Bert Freeman"?'

'Perhaps — who knows? Where would you start looking next?'

'The Hemmingsworth office, obviously.'

'And alert them immediately to the fact that we've made the connection, enabling them to hide Mr Freeman a long way from our investigations? Try again.'

Jack thought for a moment, then gave a big smile.

'Criminal Records!'

'The gods be praised, there's hope for the boy yet. That's your job, first thing in the morning.'

'What about Hemmingsworths?'

'That's *my* job first thing in the morning.'

'Wouldn't it be less suspicious if we sent Helen or Esther in there on the pretence of making some innocent enquiry?'

'During the course of which they just happen to make reference to Bert Freeman? They aren't experienced in investigative techniques, remember, and all the indications are that someone inside Hemmingsworths has a close connection with some very dangerous people.'

'As dangerous as nicking knickers?' Jack joked.

Percy shook his head.

'My brother, and your father, was right all along when he asked me to keep a watchful eye on you. You aren't fit to be let out alone.'

'That's a bit harsh.'

'Also a bit accurate. Remember, when minimising in your own mind the actions of the elusive Mr Freeman that he also put the frighteners on quite a few women. Also, remember the convenient fate of Mr Broadhurst, the regular foreman at the joinery firm employed inside the Lamb Street building?'

'How do you mean?'

Percy tutted. 'Well you don't imagine that he accidentally fell off that ladder, do you?'

'I see,' Jack conceded. 'So now where?'

Percy looked back at the joinery office window.

'I think we've spent long enough standing here to ensure that Mr Jenston needs to change his underwear. The light in there's been off ever since we left, but men with chrome domes shouldn't stand where their shininess attracts a glare from a street lamp. Come on, Jack, let's go and visit your fiancée with the depressing news.'

'I hope you aren't here for an early supper,' Esther said, smiling, as she leaned forward to kiss Jack after opening the door to them. 'But come in anyway and tell me how your investigations are going.'

'South,' Percy announced as he stepped inside behind Jack.

'I'm sorry?' Esther enquired in search of an explanation of Percy's cryptic answer.

'South,' he repeated. 'Our investigations are going south at considerable speed. Put in less vernacular terms, we haven't been able to locate, or even identify, your Mr Freeman.'

'He's not *my* Mr Freeman.' Esther shuddered slightly as she led the way upstairs. 'I can give you tea and toasted muffins, if you don't mind the absence of butter.'

'Not if you've got jam, or even honey.' Percy smiled. 'But that's not why we're here.'

'Certainly not in my case.' Jack grinned as he acquired another kiss once they reached the kitchen.

'Have you found a wedding dress yet, Esther?' Percy asked.

Esther and Jack exchanged guilty looks before Esther replied, 'Let's just say I'm working on it.'

'And Jack tells me that you've bought a house.'

'A set of second floor rooms in Clerkenwell, actually. They need a lot of work done on them, so we got them for a good price, but we'll have to devote a lot of time in the next few months to decorating, before we buy any new furniture.'

'You'll also need to find a new bridesmaid,' Percy advised them both. 'Lucy thinks she may be expecting, in which case she'll be looking like a walking airship by the date of the wedding.'

'How do you know?' Jack asked.

'She confided in me while I was round there last week. When I was in Holborn the first time, interviewing Lillian Beckwith, I took a slight diversion in order to take a sneaky gander at where she and Teddy have set up home. He's got this very impressive set of ground floor rooms from which he conducts his architectural practice and they've converted the upper two floors into a residence. I was only there briefly the first time, but she invited me for afternoon tea last week and it was then that she told me she thinks she might be pregnant.'

'I really *must* call on her,' Esther said. 'I've not been able to have a real conversation with her for ages, given that all the talk around the Sunday dinner tables in Barking are dominated by Lady Enright. The last time Lucy and I had a decent chat was just before we waved them off on their honeymoon.'

'Paris,' Jack reminded them grumpily. 'She went to Paris and we get to go to Southend.'

'This conversation is heading in *quite* the wrong direction,' Esther interrupted. 'I presume that you're here to report on the southbound direction of your enquiries?'

'Partly, and partly to enlist your assistance.'

'Tell me the first "partly" first,' Esther requested as her eyes lit up. 'Save the good bit for later, since I'm getting pretty bored here, day after day, watching the Alliance go what you would presumably call "south".'

Percy's face took on a more serious tone as he explained what they had discovered earlier that day.

'It will probably come as no great surprise to you to learn that Mr Freeman was not a regular member of the workforce at the joinery firm that did the alterations in here. He was what we call in the trade a "plant" — a "cuckoo in the nest", to use the more general expression. He was introduced by your landlords, Hemmingsworth Properties, and I can only assume that his real role was to spy on the activities of the Alliance and report back to whoever was paying him handsomely for his services. His services as both a joinery foreman and a burglar, that is.'

'I remembered something the other day that may be helpful,' Esther chipped in. 'While the men were here, my temporary membership list went missing for the best part of two days. It had all the names and addresses of the Alliance members on it and now that you tell me that the man calling himself "Freeman" was an imposter, that explains how he knew which of the members to pay a visit to.'

'Yes,' Percy agreed, 'but it doesn't explain how he knew about the ones he visited *before* that list went missing, or how he knew which ones were of particular importance to Helen and her Alliance. Do you happen to know if anything was stolen from Helen's house when she suffered her own break-in?'

'No idea, but I could ask her. You'd have to hope so, because otherwise it means that someone very close to her is in cahoots with Mr Freeman.'

Percy turned to Jack.

'When you marry this lady, get her to give you lessons in logical deduction. As a seamstress turned accounts manager she makes a very good detective.'

Esther smiled proudly.

'So what did the joinery people tell you about Bert Freeman?'

'Slightly less than nothing, directly. But it left me in no doubt that a trade union of some sort may be behind all this. It was some sort of woodworker's union that instructed the joinery firm to allow Freeman to pose as the foreman on the job in here and he was supplied by Hemmingsworths.'

'So the real people behind this are our own landlords?' Esther queried.

Percy nodded. 'Probably, but behind them is this shadowy union whose name we don't even know yet, even less where it can be found.'

'Again, Helen may be able to help with that,' Esther suggested. 'Now, what is it you want me to do?'

'You have the names and addresses of all your current Alliance members?' Percy asked.

Esther nodded. 'Of course — that's my job.'

'Well, I want you to pay a visit to as many of them as you can. Not just the ones who lost an item of underwear and not even just the ones who only got a warning that you know about. There's a distinct possibility that more of your members also got a warning, but chose to ignore it. What we're looking for is anyone among them who can give us a closer lead to the man calling himself Bert Freeman. I'd be surprised if he wasn't already known to at least one of them, probably somewhere in the East End. Your job is to find that one.'

'You realise that we still have over seven hundred members and that not all of them live in the East End, or even London?' Esther objected.

'Did I say it would be easy?' Percy smiled sympathetically. 'Jack and I could obviously call on them all, but we each have other lines of enquiry to pursue and the women are more likely to talk more freely to you. Added to which, we don't want to scare away from membership any women who haven't yet had a visit, so it's a delicate matter.'

'And you trust me with it?'

'Of course,' Percy replied. 'I've never forgotten how you charmed Pearly Poll into admitting that she carried out abortions.'

'And nearly got herself killed in the process!' Jack objected. 'I can't let you do this, Esther.'

Esther smiled back with sweet sarcasm.

'You forget that you're talking to a lady associated with a women's union. If I've learned anything from Helen, it's that women are not simply on this earth to be told by men what they can and cannot do. Your concern is noted, Jack, but stick it up your waistcoat.'

'I don't like what Esther's turning into,' Jack muttered darkly to Percy as they walked towards the bus stop half an hour later.

'I do.' Percy grinned. 'Before much longer she'll even be a worthy opponent for your mother.'

Chapter 15

The following morning, well before nine o'clock, Percy had already been given a polite brush off by two people on the staff of Hemmingsworth Properties. The first was Samuel Hemmingsworth himself, who assured him that the rental side of the business was entirely the province of his fellow director Timothy Bowden, but that if he cared to take a seat in the outer office, Mr Bowden would no doubt be able to deal with his enquiry. Back in the outer office, an early middle-aged lady who had probably missed her true calling as a bricklayer's labourer advised him bluntly that "Mr Timothy" was not in the habit of attending the office until at least ten o'clock in the morning, but that if he'd care to take a seat…

Percy sat twiddling the rim of his pork pie hat in his hands as he watched the daily ritual begin in the outer office. The bricklaying lady made a big fuss of ensuring that all the brochures were properly displayed on the front counter before retreating behind a desk that looked even smaller with her impressive bulk behind it, removed the cover from a typewriter that looked more like an offensive weapon in her hands and began attacking it with enough manual force to make the table underneath it shake with foreboding.

The lady then rose to her feet when a younger woman scuttled in with a sad saga regarding a collision between a cab and a milk float at Ludgate Circus, to which she responded with a long homily on the virtues of leaving for work early 'just in case'. Her manner was noticeably more friendly when a dapper little man sporting what must have been the only winged collar visible in Hoxton at that early hour, if at all, slipped through the front door as if anxious to avoid being seen by the lady committing cruel and unnatural offences against the typewriter. But he was apprehended just before he made it to the door of the inner office.

'A gentleman here to see you, Mr Bowden. He wouldn't specify the nature of his business,' she added, making it sound like a matter for grave suspicion.

'Do come in,' Bowden invited Percy and he dodged past the eyebrow artillery of the office turnkey and stepped inside, where he took the proffered seat in front of the large desk almost completely covered in brochures of various kinds.

'What can I do for you, Mr —?'

'Enright. Percy Enright. The business premises at 27 Lamb Street, Spitalfields?'

The man's eyes glassed over as he pretended to think for a moment.

'Ah yes — the ones that used to be a tailor's workshop? I'm afraid they're currently under lease.'

'By a lady called Helen Trenchard, who's in the process of forming an Alliance of female workers,' Percy reminded him, watching the sudden undulations of the man's larynx with satisfaction.

'What she's using the premises for precisely is none of our business,' Bowden replied evasively and Percy mentally celebrated his second hit. 'Assuming it's legal, of course.'

'Of course,' Percy agreed. 'But I was wondering if you could supply me with further information regarding the workmen who recently carried out internal alterations in there.'

If the larynx moved much faster it could be used to power a textile mill, Percy concluded as he watched Bowden compose his first evasive answer.

'It's a firm we use regularly for work of that kind,' Bowden assured him. 'I can give you their office address, if you're seeking to engage them on some work of your own. They're based in Bow, from memory.'

'I know,' Percy took mild delight in advising him, 'I was there yesterday.'

'Then I'm really not sure what further assistance I can render,' Bowden replied as the first light film of sweat appeared above his eyebrows.

'It's a rather delicate and awkward matter,' Percy continued as he tried his best to look embarrassed. 'My niece is employed by the Alliance that occupies that building and she was unwise enough to lend a modest amount of money to the man who was in charge of the other workmen. Then he simply didn't turn up for work again and my niece is anxious to secure the return of the money. As I said, the amount is modest enough, but my niece has strong Christian principles and I'm sure I need not underline her desire to ensure that the debt is repaid.'

'Quite, and it proves the old adage about being neither a borrower nor a lender,' Bowden agreed unctuously, 'but presumably you were able to obtain some sort of assistance from the man's employers?'

'No, regrettably not.' Percy smiled deceivingly as he moved in for the killer punch. 'And that's why I'm here, at the suggestion of Eastside Jobbers and Joiners. They tell me that the man who supervised the work on the Lamb Street premises was supplied by your company. This *is* a registered company, is it not? Only Mr Hemmingsworth referred to you as his "fellow director". Clearly you don't entirely disapprove of borrowing money from investors?'

'Who exactly *are* you?' Bowden demanded weakly, as his face approached ashen in hue.

'A concerned uncle, as I advised you,' Percy replied as blandly as he could to cover his elation. 'But who exactly are *you?*'

'I believe that this consultation is at an end,' Bowden insisted as he rose from his chair.

'You can believe that if you like,' Percy gloated back. 'But take it from me, there'll be others.'

Chapter 16

'I do apologise for dropping in on you like this,' Esther said, smiling warmly at Lucy over the china tea cup, 'but I simply had to come over here and congratulate you on what I believe may be a happy event in the near future. Also, to get some decorating ideas — you're so artistic.'

Lucy smiled artlessly.

'Uncle Percy always did have a big mouth. But please don't let Mother know — I want to tell her in my own time and I'm not entirely certain yet. I have an appointment with a man in Devonshire Street next week then I'll know for sure. If I'm correct, then of course I'll step down from being your bridesmaid, because the child will be due in August and I'll look hideous by June.'

'Have you told Teddy yet?'

'Of course, since he was the cause of it. He's delighted, fortunately, but it's a bit inconvenient for my budding acting career. I've joined this amateur theatre group just up the road and I was hoping to audition for the lead in "Saint Joan". Even though it's being put on in April, my bulging side profile even then would not quite be suitable for the Maid of Orleans.'

'If you aren't to be bridesmaid, no doubt your mother will insist that you hand over the role to one or more of your cousins. Which ones should I avoid?'

'Angelica, most certainly. If ever a girl didn't live up to her name, it's her — the family's resident practical joker. You'd be almost guaranteed frogs down your bodice, ants in your underwear and one of her home-made "windy blasters" under the groom's seat in the church. And avoid her sister Clarissa, who cries buckets at anything, including her own parents' wedding anniversary on one legendary occasion.'

'It might be best if I name my own choices,' Esther chuckled. 'Who's left?'

'Aunt Jane's two would be a safe bet,' Lucy advised her. 'Alice is a very mature eleven year old and she exercises a most sensible influence over her younger sister Elizabeth, who's eight and very cute. But don't you have friends of your own, or young female relatives?'

'Even if I did, would your mother entertain them?' Esther smiled.

Lucy grinned back. 'I take your point. She does rather tend to take over and organise things. If she'd been in charge of the Hundred Years War it would have been over by the second day, with everyone joining her for a hand of bridge.'

Esther burst out laughing and wanted to throw her arms around her hostess out of sheer pleasure at being back in her company.

It fell silent for a moment, before Lucy asked, 'So how are all the other arrangements going?'

'Swimmingly. We've bought a place to live — a second floor suite of rooms in Clerkenwell which we have to start decorating and furnishing soon. Hopefully I can move in there if my current job folds up, which it looks like doing.'

'What's this glum news about your job?'

'It's all a bit complicated, but my current employer's trying to form a women's union and is meeting a good deal of resistance from some men's unions. It's all getting a bit unpleasant and I think that she'll give up soon. Then the premises will be re-let and I'll be out in the street. My continued residence in Lamb Street goes with the job, you see.'

'I'm sure we could always squeeze you in here,' Lucy offered.

Esther shook her head with a smile. 'Thanks, but as I already mentioned, I'm pushing Jack to get the new house ready so that I can live there if necessary.'

'My big brother doesn't push easily when it comes to practical matters, as you've probably discovered for yourself,' Lucy said, smiling, 'but the offer's always there, anyway.'

'Actually,' Esther responded tentatively, 'there *is* one thing.'

'Yes?'

'My wedding dress. Could I bring it here to store before the big day?'

'You've bought it already?'

'No. Actually ... look, please don't tell your mother, but I'm making it myself. It's almost finished.'

'Really? How clever of you! But then, of course, you were always so skilled at needlework and suchlike. Why can't you tell Mother — she'd be *so* proud!'

'And she'd no doubt broadcast it to the entire church congregation, in that case. But my fear is that she'll think it's a cheap and nasty way to do things. You *do* hear of working-class girls getting married in home-made sacks, or their big sister's cast-offs and your mother's so ... well, so ...'

'Say no more, Esther,' Lucy chuckled. 'Your secret's safe with me. But bring the dress over whenever you wish — I simply can't wait to see it! Another salmon sandwich?'

An hour later Esther waited for the bus at the corner of Chancery Lane bathed in the warm glow that came from being a one-time orphan who'd found a welcoming family. Then her spirits sank as she remembered what she had to start doing the following day.

Chapter 17

Percy Enright had a familiar glint in his eye as he returned from the offices of Hemmingsworth Properties and headed straight for Records, where he called for the file for the company he now suspected beyond any reasonable doubt was up to its Memorandum of Association in union money. Sure enough, there it was, so far as he could deduce given the inadequacies of the law on such matters.

Trade unions were regarded in law as 'unincorporated associations', which gave them both advantages and disadvantages from a legal perspective. Since they were not legal 'entities' they could not own property, or make investments, in their own name, but had to do so through certain nominees. These nominees were private individuals who in the case of unions could be expected to be office bearers and Percy was prepared to bet a substantial sum of money that the 'Union of Allied Woodworkers and Turners', of which a Mr George Manners was the General Secretary and legal officer, was the same union to whom a certain Mr Jenston had been referring as the one that he dared not annoy if he was to retain his job at Eastside Jobber and Joiners. The self-same union that had taken a substantial shareholding in Hemmingsworth Properties less than a year ago.

It all slotted into place as neatly as a tongue and groove joint executed by one of Eastside's skilled craftsmen. The union had invested in the property company to whom its directors were therefore beholden. By virtue of its control over the men who formed its workforce that same union was able to flex its muscle when it came to which man did which job. It was the union that had been in the ultimate overall position to ensure that when Helen Trenchard was unwittingly unwise enough to require certain internal alterations to her rented premises, it could insert its own ferret into the rabbit hole.

But was it simply a matter of union rivalry, or was there something much deeper that had not so far surfaced? And was the man who went by the name of Bert Freeman simply an unpleasant bully boy hired for the occasion, or did he have a relationship with the union — or perhaps one of its officers — that went back much further in time? Perhaps something more personal in relation to Helen herself? Though surely, if that were the case, would she not have recognised him when he was posing as the foreman inside her business premises?

One thing was clear — they were not going to get any further unless and until they could pull the mask of anonymity from the face of 'Bert Freeman'.

Though Esther had been detailed the painstaking work of enquiring of as many of her union members as she could whether any of them had something to offer that would identify the man, any name that her searches revealed would almost certainly not be that of Bert Freeman and Jack would need to be ready to match any other name that floated to the surface with a criminal history that fitted the bill. Except he had to work backwards, by unearthing likely suspects with suitable criminal histories and compiling a list of names, one of which would hopefully match the one — if any — that Esther came up with. Percy reminded himself ruefully that an easier task might be turning water into wine, or feeding the five thousand. At least he could feed two and he asked the Records Supervisor if Jack might be found inside the rabbit warren that lay behind the main desk with its many reading rooms.

'He's been in A5 since this morning,' Percy was told and he grinned as he looked through the glass panel set into the top of the door to where he could see his nephew's head bent over a pile of paper the height of a water hydrant.

'Any luck?' Percy enquired breezily as he opened the door and strolled in.

Jack rubbed his eyes and looked round.

'You wouldn't believe how many men in London remove ladies' underwear.' He grinned. 'Of course, these are just the ones who did so without encouragement from the ladies to whom they belonged.'

'How many used violence when caught in the act?'

'This smaller pile to the right here,' Jack muttered. 'I use the term "smaller" advisedly, since there are over fifty of those, just in the Met.'

'Do their criminal histories give their occupations?'

Jack gave a rueful frown. 'If they were gainfully employed they wouldn't be lags, would they? And they wouldn't have time to patrol clotheslines during drying hours.'

'Forget the clothesline specialists,' Percy instructed him. 'We're looking for a break and enter expert who has a thing for underwear and can get violent if caught at it. If you get one who lists his occupation as "joiner", that's a bonus.'

'Do you imagine I didn't already think of that?' Jack smirked. 'Here's your best four.'

From his left hand side he passed up a single sheet of paper bearing four names, behind which he had secured the relevant criminal histories with a pin. Percy studied the fruits of an entire morning's work carefully, then offered his observations.

'Brady never operated north of the river and Canavan seems to have specialised in the West End. Only Jamieson and Prescott travelled widely afield and Prescott has previous for flashing and groping, before he took to assault. But he's got no occupation listed and he should still be inside, according to this.'

'It's real needle in haystack stuff,' Jack complained.

Percy smiled. 'Welcome to the Met. Let me buy you a mutton pie.'

Downstairs and across the road, Percy brought Jack up to date with his latest findings and Jack smiled grimly when advised that the property company could be directly linked with an appropriate trade union to which it owed a big favour.

'It also ties in with what Jenston told us about not falling out with a union,' he observed, 'but what next?'

'We need to speak to Helen again. I'm hoping she can tell us something more about the man who runs this union that seems to be behind it all — George Manners. Finish that pie, then it's back down to Spitalfields.'

Helen frowned as she looked up from the desk she had placed, somewhat hopefully, in front of the reception wall that proudly displayed a new Alliance banner, but smiled when she saw Percy and Jack walking in.

'I've had dinner, I'm afraid.'

'So have we,' Percy announced, 'but a cup of tea would be nice. Then I hope you can tell me all about George Manners.'

'Where's Esther?' Jack asked as they established themselves around the kitchen table.

'She's out visiting members, as you requested,' Helen replied. 'At least, I hope you did, because that's where she's been for the past two days.'

'Has she had any luck?' Percy asked.

'Not that she's mentioned,' Helen replied, 'but I thought you were here about George Manners?'

'Is he a familiar?' Percy asked in his strange Scotland Yard manner of speech.

'Not as familiar as he'd like to be,' Helen replied through firmly set lips. 'He's a drip who hangs around hoping that I'll be overawed by his greasy charm. He's pathetic, that's all. Why, do you suspect him of some involvement in all that's been happening?'

'Most definitely,' Percy confirmed. 'He's the man who's listed as the General Secretary of the Union of Allied Woodworkers and Turners — have I got the right George Manners?'

'I think that's what he eventually called his union.' Helen nodded. 'It was formed a couple of years ago and I met him and his lady friend at a Congress meeting around the time when I was forming the Alliance. I misguidedly asked him for advice on the necessary legal and administrative steps I needed to take and then I simply couldn't shake him off. I believe that he was more interested in me personally and most of the actual advice I received came from this woman who was always there like a bad smell around an open sewer cover. It was your typical love triangle, if you can believe for one moment that a thirty-five year old like me is still capable of attracting admirers. He was pursuing me, while this woman — Margaret Templeton — was avidly pursuing him.'

'I could well understand why a man would find you sufficiently alluring to reject the advances of another woman,' Percy oozed.

Helen went bright red and opted to keep the conversation more general. 'I really couldn't imagine George Manners being a burglar, or even employing one,' she insisted.

Percy inclined his head from side to side. 'It always turns out to be the quiet ones, in my experience. May I take it that you didn't encourage Mr Manners' attentions?'

'I most certainly didn't,' Helen bristled, 'but that didn't seem to dampen his ardour. He kept sending flowers and penning letters dripping with sentiment and flattery. Almost child-like, but always beautifully scripted.'

'Definitely not the man who left that note on your bedroom wall, then?'

'Most definitely not. His letters to me were nowhere near as crude and were much better spelt.'

'He could have been deliberately trying to appear semi-literate,' Jack suggested.

Helen shook her head. 'The man who was in my room smelt of hospitals, whereas George Manners always smelt of men's pomade. Quite "Nancy", in a way, if you get my meaning.'

'A "Mary-Anne"?' Jack suggested.

Percy shook his head. 'Unlikely. The underwear nonsense was designed to instil fear, not create a private collection.'

'What's a "Mary-Anne"?' Helen enquired.

'Basically a homosexual, but one who delights in wearing women's clothing,' Percy advised her.

'So have you revised your opinion of policemen?' Jack asked quickly, registering Helen's shocked expression.

Helen smiled. 'I told Esther that I'd reserve judgment until I'd met you and you certainly haven't disappointed me. As for your lovely uncle here, well Esther was right when she said what a credit he was to the Metropolitan Police and how comforting it was just to have him around.'

Percy managed to look embarrassed, Jack suppressed a smirk and Helen blushed again, but they all saved further awkwardness when they heard the faint sound of a key being turned in the front door lock downstairs.

'Ah, that sounds like Esther returning,' Helen announced with a slightly overdone breeziness. 'Let's see if she's got anything to tell us.'

Esther's glum face lightened as she entered the kitchen and saw Jack and Percy in attendance. She kissed Jack, then sat down heavily.

'Any tea left? And perhaps a large brandy?'

'Was it so bad?' Jack enquired solicitously as he put his arm around her.

'Worse,' Esther announced as she reached for a ginger biscuit. 'If I have to visit one more hovel full of screaming children, women with wet washing hanging from their ceilings and the ever-present smell of overflowing privies, I swear I'll become a nun instead.'

'We can't have that,' Jack chuckled.

Percy looked enquiringly into her eyes. 'What my shallow nephew should have asked was whether or not your displeasure is caused by lack of progress.'

'You could put it that way,' Esther nodded with exhausted eyes, 'but it's the sheer depression of it all. The women who haven't received any warning are suspicious of my motives for calling, the ones who have can't get me out of their rooms fast enough, and nobody seems to know of a man in the woodworking trade who has an eye for ladies' undergarments. Apart from their own men, of course. I'm up to my neck in lurid stories of how their menfolk seduce them into yet more childbirth, then head off to the pub.'

'Typical men!' Helen muttered, then turned with an apologetic look at Percy and Jack. 'Present company excepted, of course.'

'This clearly isn't working,' Percy announced unnecessarily. 'How many women do you think you've spoken to now?'

'Perhaps twenty, in the two days I've been doing it. Many of them were at work when I called, so I'll obviously have to chase them up on Saturdays, making Sunday dinner at Enright Palace the highlight of my week, when it coincides with one of Jack's days off.'

Percy tapped his lips with his fingers, a habitual habit of his when thinking deeply.

'Perhaps you should concentrate on the ones who we know got a visit. Pretend that you're a concerned Alliance officer who's trying to coax them back. Give them oodles of sympathy and see what drops out in casual conversation.'

'I've done a couple of those already,' Esther protested. 'Have you ever tried to have a casual conversation with a woman whose private accommodation was entered without leaving any trace, whose most intimate garments were violated and who was left with two threatening notes, one of them obscene? Every door I managed to get through was opened an inch or two first by a terrified wretch who thought it might be the intruder returning to have their wicked way with her.'

'I know the feeling,' Helen confirmed with a shudder. 'Ever since the forced entry to my house I've never felt safe. Some nights I lie awake at night waiting for the sound of an intruder — you wouldn't believe how many naturally creaking floorboards one house can have.'

Percy's eyes opened wider as a thought struck him.

'You never found any indication of how the intruder got in?'

'No. I examined the front door carefully straight after it happened, but there were no signs of any attempt to force it — no "jemmy" marks, as I believe they're called.'

'I'd like to examine your door for myself, if I may,' Percy replied. 'It might help to narrow the ground in identifying the man responsible to know whether or not he was armed with skeleton keys.'

'What on earth are those?' Helen enquired.

'Keys that work on any lock of the type they're made to fit,' Jack advised her, not wishing to be left out of the intelligence exchange. 'Only certain types of burglar use them. I think what Uncle Percy's getting at is that if a skeleton key was used, then we can narrow the search down to professional burglars, rather than amateurs who got lucky.'

'He can't have got lucky all those times, surely?' Esther argued.

Percy nodded. 'As usual, Esther my dear, a very intelligent observation.'

'Please don't call me "my dear",' Esther responded huffily. 'It's so patronising and it reminds me of your sister-in-law.'

'Sorry about that, but the compliment was well meant. Even with skeleton keys you need to be bypassing the type of lock that it was designed for, but from my experience the locks on the individual doors inside rooming houses are of all types, some better than others. Some are so weak that a smart kick will do the trick, yet not a single one of our victims reported a broken door frame.'

'So?' Jack enquired, genuinely mystified.

'So our man has a different way of getting in and I think it may be connected with the putty that was used to stick the warning notices up. Hence my interest in Helen's front door.'

'Would tomorrow be convenient? I normally go shopping on Saturday mornings, but if you arrive at, say, one o'clock, I can have some dinner ready for you. It'll make a nice change to be preparing a meal for two instead of just one.'

'Could we make that three?' Jack asked politely.

'Yes, of course, if you'd like to tag along as well,' Helen replied.

'Not so much a matter of "tagging along" as learning something new,' Jack said with an engaging smile directed at Percy. 'After all, I *am* attached to the Burglary section within the Yard and I could benefit from learning about new methods of unlawful entry.'

'I didn't realise that you were so keen to learn the tricks of the trade,' Percy commented as they stood waiting for the bus a few minutes later.

'I'm not,' Jack replied with a grin. 'I'll be representing Aunt Beattie — just in case.'

Chapter 18

Esther climbed wearily up her final staircase for the day, to the top floor of the common lodging house in Walpole Street, Wapping, inconveniently located between the noise and soot of the railway and the smell from the river. She stepped daintily around the children playing marbles on the top landing with a set of round polished stones that looked as if they had been collected from the river bank and reached out to tap on the door of number seventeen. Curiously, and unusually, it was unlocked and swung in lightly as she knocked, revealing the sight of a girl little past her teens leaning over a crib of some sort in an attempt to pacify an infant that was whimpering quietly inside it.

'Come in, Wally, it's on the latch,' the girl called out, then stood upright and looked round when there was no response. 'Who the 'ell are you?' she demanded.

Slightly embarrassed, Esther smiled reassuringly as she replied: 'My name's Esther Jacobs and I'm from the National Women's Labour Alliance.'

'I ain't a member o' that no more,' the girl insisted.

'I know and that's why I'm here,' Esther replied. 'May I come in?'

'If yer must, but me man'll be back in a mo an' 'e don't take kindly ter visitors on 'is days off.'

'You *are* Tilly Chalmers, I take it?'

'Yeah, that's me.'

'I'm here to enquire about your reason for leaving the Alliance, Miss Chalmers.'

'None o' yer bloomin' business.'

'Of course it's not, in the sense that it was your decision. But we seem to be losing quite a few members recently and we were wondering if the fault lies with us, or if there's some other reason.'

Tilly looked hard at the entrance door to the single room.

'I come 'ome one day ter find the door bust open an' all me clothes flung around the room. Some o' them 'ad bin stolen an' all — like *personal* fings, if yer gets me meanin'.'

'You mean your underwear?'

'Yeah. 'As there bin others?'

'Yes, quite a few. Did the person responsible by any chance leave you a note?'

'Yeah, but it meant nowt ter me, 'cos I can't read proper. But me man Wally, 'e read it ter me an' it said as 'ow if I stayed in that union, I'd get me face cut open. I weren't goin' ter risk that, not wi' a baby ter look after. That's 'im in the cot there — Tommy. But fortunately 'e were wi' me neighbour across the landin' — Mrs Tasker, that's 'er name. She always looks after 'im while I'm out workin' at the fish dock an' Tommy were safely wi' 'er when the burglar called.'

'And the door to your room had been forced, you say?'

'Yeah, it 'ad. Whoever it were took a jemmy or summat ter the wood at the side an' the door musta just popped open.'

'It looks alright now, though,' Esther commented as she looked back towards it. 'You must have got it repaired.'

'Yeah, me man did that. 'Cept 'e weren't me man then. I were told about this bloke what lives down the street what fixes doors an' things an' 'e come an' replaced the wood. That's why the door's still cream, but the frame at the side ain't been painted yet. 'Im an' me took a fancy ter each other an' now 'e's ter be found 'ere most nights. 'E's fair taken ter little Tommy, so that's alright, an' me an' 'im's thinkin' o' maybe gettin' 'itched once the weather gets warmer. Are yer married yerself?'

'Not quite, but I will be after June,' Esther replied, feeling desperately ashamed of the splendid ceremony she'd be given in a country parish church, compared with the brief registry office process in which this unfortunate young innocent would commit her body, her devotion, and her pathetic weekly wage to some wastrel who'd move on once the novelty wore off, no doubt leaving another infant or two in his wake.

'So your man — Wally? — fixed your door for you?' Esther enquired, intrigued that this break-in seemed different from the others.

'Yeah, that's right — an' 'e read me the note an' all.'

'Do you still have the note?'

'Nah, Wally threw it away 'cos it were that upsettin' fer me.'

'But you saw it before he threw it away?'

'Course I did — weren't yer listenin'? It were lyin' in the bubby's cot — 'cept the bubby weren't in it, like I said.'

'Can you remember what the note looked like?'

'Why all the questions? You wi' the Peelers or somefin'?'

'No, but as I said, the Alliance which I represent has sent me to find out as much as we can about who's been threatening our members.'

'Well, it were just a piece o' paper, like yer see on noticeboards an' suchlike. An' it were printed, like it were in a newspaper.'

'Just the one message?'

'That's what it looked like ter me. An' how many times does it take ter warn somebody that they're gonna get their face cut open?'

'Thank you *very* much, Miss Chalmers, you've been a great help. And all the best for your wedding.'

'An' good luck wi' yourn. Thanks fer not tryin' ter get me back inter that union — it's more than me life's worth. An' chances are that Wally wouldn't fancy me any more, wi' me face carved open. Yer can see yerself out, can yer? Only bubby's started cryin' again.'

Esther stood outside on the pavement, thinking deeply, as Saturday shoppers walked past her in both directions, carrying groceries that no doubt had to last them until the next pay day, if there was one. She shuddered to think that only some guardian angel had preserved her from a life like this, as she made her way down to the main road, where the bus would take her back up to Lamb Street, on the Liverpool Street service that stopped outside her door.

She could barely contain her excitement as she pieced together all that she had just learned from Tilly Chalmers. A different mode of entry that had made it possible for a man named Wally to visit her and carry out the necessary repairs that marked him out as a man skilled in woodworking. The usual plundering and theft of undergarments, but no obscene note in woodworker's pencil, almost as if the intruder knew that Tilly was illiterate anyway. And the threat itself, which according to this Wally was nothing like the others. The threat to Tilly was far more violent in its terms and this also marked it out as a different sort of attack on an Alliance member. A woman in Tilly's position living with that sort of threat would be only too willing to trade her body for the physical protection of a man.

Something else was nagging at Esther's mind as well, but she couldn't quite put her finger on it. Then her conscious brain shifted with a jerk into another mode as she looked down the bus queue and there, only several people away, was Bert

Freeman. She hoped that her face didn't betray the shock as she waved half-heartedly towards him in a 'Do I know you?' sort of way and he nodded back formally. The bus drew up a few moments later and Esther took a seat near the downstairs front, allowing herself only a brief glance to confirm that Freeman was also on the bus, a few seats behind her and staring fixedly out of the window as they rattled and swayed north across Whitechapel Road.

Any remaining hope she might have entertained that he would get off somewhere in Whitechapel were dashed fifteen minutes later when she passed him as she moved down the bus to the platform from which she alighted onto the busy pavement across the road from the Alliance headquarters. She dared not look behind her, but instead glanced from the corner of her eye at a movement to her right as she pretended to be selecting a safe moment to scuttle across the road between the carriages and carts that formed a constant stream up and down Lamb Street. There was someone crossing at the same time, but was it Freeman?

Breathlessly she fiddled in her handbag for her front door key, conscious that her building was empty on a Saturday. Once the key was safely in the lock, but before turning it, she looked swiftly behind her and there he was, leering stupidly at her.

'I *thought* it were you, Miss, but I weren't sure. What a coincidence, you bein' down Wappin' way an' in the same buildin' what me missus lives in.'

'Why did you follow me?' Esther demanded with as much authority as her quavering breathlessness would allow.

'I *weren't* followin' yer, in the sense you means.' Freeman smiled back reassuringly. 'It's just a case that we was both goin' in the same direction ter the same place. I was wonderin' if I left me best 'ammer at yours when I finished that job fer yer.'

'You left your men to finish that job off and you had plenty of time to collect any lost property — at least two days. I can assure you that there's no hammer left inside there. We were very particular in cleaning the place up, after your men left all those wood shavings behind them. Good afternoon, Mr Freeman.'

She turned her back on him and swiftly turned the key in the lock, expecting at any moment that a brawny hand would grab her wrist, or pull her back from the door by her clothing. She was tensed, ready to scream her lungs empty, when the door yielded to her desperate push and she opened it enough to slide inside and slam it behind her, whimpering in fear as she leaned her full weight on the back of the door, in case he tried to kick it in. She only scuttled away from it when the urgent prompting of her bladder forced her upstairs at a run.

As she washed her hands afterwards, she remembered what had been bothering her earlier, like a gas flame bursting into life between her ears. After creeping carefully back down the stairs and checking that the front door was securely bolted, she moved through the opening into her section of the office, carrying the lamp that she needed in order to combat the rapidly descending dusk of that early February evening. A quick search of the relevant folders yielded the warning letters that she had collected from various members she had visited the previous day, two of whom had received the full treatment of stolen or disturbed underwear and a crude additional message in pencil. She shivered as she read yet again the filthy suggestions that they contained and imagined how it would feel having Freeman's hands wandering inside her most intimate apparel while they were being worn, then she forced herself to conduct the most important part of the experiment that had occurred to her.

Thankful that she had taken such great care to keep everything alphabetical, she extracted the letter of resignation allegedly written by Tilly Chalmers. A Tilly Chalmers whom she now knew to be illiterate, whose letter would almost certainly have been written for her by Wally. Like the warning letters from the other two files, it was written in thick pencil and was badly spelt.

She gave a squeal of triumph, but quickly cut it short in case anyone was listening outside. Then she crept to the darkened front window that looked out over Lamb Street and peered as far to the right and left as the window frames allowed. There were several passers-by, but no sign of Bert Freeman. With a swift prayer of thanks, followed by a further Hebrew prayer remembered from childhood that called for Yahweh's protection of the tribes of Abraham, she crept stealthily up the shadowy creaking stairs into her bedroom.

On Monday she'd get Jack to fix a bolt on the inside of her bedroom door. In the meantime, prayers would have to suffice as she dropped her outer clothes to the floor and slipped between the sheets in her undergarments, just in case. She finally fell asleep with the happy thought that tomorrow was Sunday — who would ever have imagined that she would so look forward to a Sunday dinner hosted by Constance Enright?

Chapter 19

Jack arrived half an hour early, just in case Helen had in mind inveigling Uncle Percy inside the house and plying him with charm and God knew what all else. He owed his father's brother and his wife everything, he reflected, as he leaned back on the front fence and gazed across at Victoria Park. He'd lived here in Hackney ever since his father died and Uncle Percy had kept his promise to his dearly loved older brother and taken Jack under his wing. Jack's mother had protested loudly to no avail, since Jack had always hero-worshipped his wise and worldly Police Constable uncle, a boyhood obsession that matured into respect when Percy went up through the ranks, then joined the Yard as a detective.

It had been almost inevitable that three years later Jack would choose the same profession and earn his way out of uniform in Whitechapel to join Percy as a Yard detective. This elevation owed much to the role played by them both, working as a team, in exposing the infamous Jack the Ripper and ending the spate of gruesome killings in Jack's Division. But none of that would have been possible without the street-wise, but somehow still enchantingly vulnerable, Esther — his bride to be.

'I might have known you'd be here first,' came the familiar voice to his right, as Percy walked towards him with a broad grin. 'Even though I live just a few streets away, in the house you spent your formative years in, you still contrived to make it here earlier from your lodgings in Farringdon.'

'I wanted to make sure that Miss Trenchard didn't drag you in there to a fate worse than death if Aunt Beattie found out. And why are you grinning like that?'

'On my way down Mare Street, I passed a fixed point bobby on the corner, sitting on a garden fence as if he was a gardener taking his morning tea break. I walked up to him, flashed my police badge and told him what a disgrace he was to the image of a fine force. I threatened to report him if he didn't smarten up his act and I guarantee that he'll never sit on that fence again. Now, why aren't you already examining that front door?'

'I thought I'd leave that to you. And I didn't want to be seen to be acting suspiciously.'

'That possibility obviously didn't concern whoever gained access to Miss Trenchard's house. Are we sure we've got the right address?'

Jack checked his notebook, then peered down the front path at the number on the front door.

'Number 64 — that seems to be the one.'

'Right, follow me, constable.'

They walked in file, Percy in the lead, down the front garden path that ran past a few winter-skeletal rose bushes on either side and reached the front door without challenge. Percy first examined its side frames, in case Helen had missed something significant, then rattled the handle below the keyhole. When that revealed nothing suspicious he peered carefully into the keyhole itself. With a sigh of satisfaction he then extracted a small eyeglass from his waistcoat pocket and peered in again. Finally, he gave a chuckle and produced a pocket knife from his jacket, which he inserted into the keyhole and twisted. Then he removed the knife and held it up in the air to reveal a minute particle of something white on its tip.

'There we are, Jack my boy. Watch and learn. Putty, if I'm not much mistaken.'

Just then the front door was opened from the inside and there stood Helen.

'It's customary to knock,' she said, smiling. 'I hope you like shepherd's pie, otherwise I'll be eating it for a week. Do come inside. I take it that you weren't using that knife to replicate a break-in?'

'Yes and no,' Percy replied enigmatically. 'Do you by any chance recall receiving a visit on a day prior to the break-in, by a man offering to clean your windows or fix your roof or something?'

'Not that I can recall, why?'

'It's an old dodge,' Percy advised her as he helped himself to a three day supply of shepherd's pie. 'First they ring the bell to see if anyone answers. If not, there's a fair chance that nobody's in, so then they break in.'

'And if somebody *is* in?' Helen enquired.

'Then they just pretend to be seeking work as a gardener or something — and by the way, you should have dead-headed those roses once they stopped flowering.'

'But my break-in occurred at night, when there was obviously somebody in,' Helen objected.

Percy nodded. 'Precisely, since in your case the objective was to cause fear.'

'It certainly achieved that. But how did the man gain entry?'

'Sometime previously,' Percy advised her with a self-satisfied smile. 'This pie's delicious, by the way. Mind you, I speak as a man whose wife's cooking is fit only for prisoners on hard labour.'

'You've completely lost me,' Helen complained, 'but thank you for the compliment about my cooking.'

'Let me see if I can work it out for myself,' Jack volunteered. 'The man calls at a time when he knows you're out, probably by keeping watch from the park across the road. Then he saunters up to your door armed with a handful of putty and pushes it into the keyhole while making a pretence of knocking. He then removes the putty, with a perfect profile of your keyhole, and gets a locksmith to cut a skeleton version that he can use again, at any time of day or night. Am I right, Detective Sergeant?'

'In every detail, Detective Constable.'

Helen shivered, despite the fire blazing in the hearth.

'To think that it was that easy! And to think that he was able to creep around inside here while I was asleep — ugh!'

She put down her fork and took a long draught of her wine. Percy reached across the table with a consoling hand on hers.

'If it helps, I can almost guarantee that he won't use it again, since it's already served his purpose.'

'But he *could*, if he wanted to, couldn't he?' Helen almost moaned. 'I think it's high time I moved in with Esther.'

'I'm sure she'd be glad of the company,' Jack agreed, 'and I'd be happier in my own mind, knowing that she had company as well.'

'Sorry to spoil this excellent lunch even more,' Percy observed quietly, 'but we can almost guarantee that he's the same man who posed as Bert Freeman and that at some stage he performed the same trick on the front door of your Alliance premises. You'll obviously need to have *both* locks changed and I'll arrange for a firm of locksmiths trusted and employed by the Yard to do both jobs without delay.'

'Presumably we can now start visiting all the dodgy locksmiths on our list, asking serious questions?' Jack asked.

'Do you know how many there are?' Percy objected. 'And what about the ones who *aren't* on our list? All the failed blacksmiths, out of work welders and anyone else who can melt metal into a key?'

'Sounds pretty hopeless,' Helen agreed. 'Let's hope that Esther's having more success than on her previous enquiries.'

'Why can't you tell me *now*?' Jack pouted as he and Esther sat side by side on the train rattling east along the London, Tilbury and Essex line from Fenchurch Street for their customary Sunday dinner in Barking.

'Because I want Uncle Percy to hear it as well and you have a memory like a colander sometimes. Tell me how you went at Helen's house yesterday — did she eat Uncle Percy?'

'Not quite, but of course I was there as the representative of his conscience. I dread to think what might have transpired if I hadn't — she's a very attractive lady and fifteen or more years younger than him.'

'You think of her as very attractive?'

Jack grinned as he kissed her cheek. 'Did I make you jealous just then?'

'Yes, of course, but it gave me another thought,' Esther mused. 'Supposing this isn't about the Alliance at all, but is some sort of revenge from that union type whose attentions she rejected?'

'That's a bit of a long shot, isn't it?'

'Maybe, but let's not discount it. So did you find out how that dreadful man got into Helen's house?'

'Of course — the oldest trick in the book,' Jack breezed back in Uncle Percy's own words, hoping to make himself sound more experienced. 'A piece of putty in the keyhole that makes an impression of the key which can be used as the template for an extra one.'

'Is it really that simple?'

'Yes, and by the way, you can expect some locksmiths to appear at your Alliance office in the next few days to change your locks.'

'You mean that the same trick was performed on our front door?'

'Almost certainly.'

'Oh God!' Esther reacted as the colour drained from her face.

Jack looked anxiously across at her. 'Are you about to faint or something? Shall I open a window?'

'In *this* weather? No, I'll be alright. It's just that ... .well ...'

'Well what?'

'I was followed back to the Alliance yesterday by Bert Freeman. He didn't try to force his way in or anything, but he's worked out that I live there and if you tell me he's got a spare key...'

'Right, that's it!' Jack insisted. 'You'll have to accept Mother's well-meaning offer to move in with her.'

'And endure this awful train journey every day? Today we've got a compartment to ourselves, but I could almost guarantee that on working days it'll be full of smelly workmen. And the journey takes the best part of an hour. There are two alternatives.'

'What?'

'Well, first of all, Lucy very kindly offered to let me stay with her. That wouldn't be ideal, for either of us, but at least I'd be both safe and nearer to work. The second alternative is that you get a move on with decorating our future home, so that I can move in there well before the wedding.'

'I just remembered something,' Jack advised her. 'Helen's terrified of remaining in her house, now that she knows about the spare key, so she'll probably ask to move in with you at the Alliance.'

'Better than nothing, I suppose. But two women against a brute the size of Freeman? Or are you just trying to get out of starting the decorating?'

'First thing tomorrow I'll go shopping for wallpaper and paste,' Jack assured her.

Esther was waiting near the front door to head Percy off even before Alice had taken his hat and coat down to the hall cupboard.

'Thank God you didn't bring Aunt Beattie!' she whispered hoarsely.

'Oh come on, she's not that bad!' Percy joked with a smile.

'No, but she keeps you indoors with her and we need to talk urgently, and preferably before Jack's mother orders us to eat. Let's hide on the back lawn and leave Jack to keep Constance occupied.'

'So what's so damned urgent?' Percy demanded, slightly irritated at having to bypass the compulsory pre-lunch sherry course.

'I think I've found Bert Freeman!'

Percy's eyebrows shot up. 'Where is he and what makes you so certain?'

'Wapping, where he's living most of the time with one of his victims and a former member of the Alliance. I think he used the fear he'd induced in her to play the part of the big brave protector, since she's only a young girl with a baby and quite pretty in her own way.'

'I'll need more than that, I'm afraid,' Percy said, frowning.

'Well, try this for size,' Esther persevered. 'We got the usual resignation letter from this girl — her name's Tilly Chalmers, by the way — but I discovered while talking to her that she's illiterate, so somebody must have written that letter for her. I checked when I got back to the office and her letter's in the same capital letters, written with the same sort of pencil and containing the same spelling mistakes, as at least two of the threatening notes that the worst victims received.'

'That sounds more encouraging,' Percy conceded.

'This man that Tilly's living with — she called him Wally, which is presumably short for Walter — is skilled at working with wood. And when I was leaving Tilly's, Bert Freeman turned up out of nowhere, followed me home and conveniently confirmed that the lodging house I'd been visiting was the home of his lady friend. How about all that, then?'

'I'm very impressed. But I'm a bit concerned about Freeman following you home. If he realises that you're living there...'

'Yes, I know,' Esther interrupted. 'Jack told me all about the spare key that Freeman may have made.'

'And what was Jack's response to all your other news?'

'I haven't told him yet. Plenty of time for that. But I don't get to see you as often as I do him.'

'That's about to change,' Percy assured her. 'We need to put the buckles on Freeman without delay and I'll be the one who organises that. But first you'll need to point him out, since neither Jack nor I know what he looks like.'

'You want me to lure him out into the open?'

'Well, I wasn't exactly suggesting that you place an advertisement in the newspaper. We'll talk over the details after dinner. Right now we've both earned a sherry, before Constance hides the bottle from the cook. But well done, young lady — you're a credit to the Scotland Yard that you're not even a member of.'

'It sounds incredibly risky,' Jack objected almost two hours later, when Esther and Percy brought him up to speed on the rear lawn, after they had all been granted leave from the dinner table at which Percy had threatened to light up his pipe.

'What's so risky about it, with you and a couple of other plain-clothes types walking a few paces behind her?' Percy enquired of Jack. 'As soon as she picks him out, we can pounce.'

'Don't you want to know where he lives first?' Esther asked and Percy agreed that this would be preferable. When Jack asked why, Percy fixed him with one of his withering looks.

'Ask the other detective in the family,' he replied with a nod towards Esther, who obliged without the need for any further encouragement from Jack.

'Evidence. If he's who we think he is, his room will contain things like putty, spare keys, warning notices he hasn't yet delivered, and so on.'

'Not to mention enough ladies' underwear to stock a draper's shop,' Percy added.

'So you're proposing that Esther parade up and down the street in Wapping where he lives — an area of London with a crime rate almost as bad as Whitechapel — in the hope that she'll spot Freeman?' Jack asked, far from impressed by the suggestion.

'Do you think you could locate him faster through criminal records?' Percy challenged him.

Jack shook his head.

'At least we know his name's Walter, so on Monday I can narrow down my searches. But I'm still not happy using Esther as a magnet.'

'Get off your protective high horse, Jack,' Esther sniffed. 'I want to do it, and it's the best bit of luck we've had since we started all this.'

'You *really* should consider joining the Yard when that proposal finally goes through to appoint female officers,' Percy said admiringly.

'If she lives that long,' Jack muttered. 'But back me up on this point, Uncle Percy — Esther ought not to be living there all alone any more, now that Freeman knows she's vulnerable.'

'She won't *be* alone, if Helen keeps to her intention of moving in with her, will she?' Percy countered. 'And once we buckle Freeman, that'll be it — final whistle blown and danger removed from our midst.'

'Think it through,' Jack argued. 'The ultimate target is Helen and her union. Freeman's probably already fulfilled his function and been paid off. The Alliance shows no sign of closing yet, so what comes next? An attack on Helen's life? A fire bomb through the window? I don't want Esther exposed to any danger.'

'Neither does Esther,' the object of his concerns replied, 'and the most immediate risk of that will be if we don't go back in there and appear to be interested in all the latest gossip from the St Margaret's Ladies Guild. Stifle the yawns and no more talk of protecting Esther from her inexplicable desire to save other women from being terrorised in their own homes.'

Chapter 20

The next week passed uneventfully on all fronts. Jack had the Tuesday and Wednesday off, due to the routine switch in duty rosters, and Helen was more than happy for Esther to take a break from the paperwork, being well aware that she was always on top of it anyway, so they were free to make a start on decorating. Their first port of call was a hardware store in Clerkenwell High Street, where they bought a large tin of white oil-based paint, several different size brushes, a scrubbing brush, a bucket and a collection of cleaning cloths. Then it was back to their intended matrimonial home with light hearts and, shortly afterwards in what would one day be their kitchen, stomachs full of the bread and cheese, washed down with bottled ginger beer, that they'd brought in with them.

Jack lay back contentedly on the bare boards but Esther was back on her feet.

'Now, let's heat up some water and get on with scrubbing and washing down the doors. Good thing the lady who died here left us the gas stove.'

'She won't be needing it anyway,' Jack called out. 'Where do you want to start?'

'In here,' she shouted through from another room. 'It'll be our bedroom. If I'm going to move in before the wedding I'll need this room ready, if nothing else.'

'You're still determined to live in the Alliance building in the meantime?'

'Of course. The rat we're planning to catch trades on fear and if I move out I'm only letting him succeed with me in the same way that he succeeded with all those other women. I can do better than that.'

Jack put his arm over her shoulder, then let it drift downwards as he reached round and kissed her on the lips.

'I'm *so* frightened of losing you, Esther. The sooner you move in here, the happier I'll be.'

'And the sooner we get this room ready, the sooner I can move in. So stop wasting time and pick up that scrubbing brush!'

'How are the home decorations going?' Helen enquired over morning tea on the Thursday.

Esther smiled at the memory. 'They'd progress a lot faster if Jack would concentrate on the decorating, if you get my meaning.'

'Indeed I do.' Helen grinned. 'I haven't always been without an admirer, you know. And there are times that I wish I'd not rejected so many of them when it came to a marriage proposal. I collected four over the years, but something always held me back from making a commitment.'

'When I see the conditions that some of our members are living in after making just such a commitment, it almost puts *me* off. But somehow with Jack, it feels right, and I can't imagine life without him, so I suppose I'll have to look forward to children and domestic duties one day not too far in the future.'

'There are days I'd gladly welcome that,' Helen said. 'Particularly at the moment, when living alone in a rambling three storey house gets a bit creepy, knowing that Freeman's out there with a spare key.'

'Jack said that you were thinking of moving in here. You can have my room, if you like and I'll take the room on the top floor that I used to occupy when Isaac and his wife adopted me.'

'That's very generous of you and I probably will, as soon as I can sell the house in Hackney. I'll have to soon to finance the Alliance, although we don't seem to have had any more cancelled memberships this week.'

'Jack and Uncle Percy seem to think that Freeman's completed his dirty work, but my worry is that since it's obviously failed, whoever's behind all this will try something worse.'

'If they're right about that,' Helen said with a frown, 'then why are you still going ahead with that rather dangerous scheme to trap Freeman and bring him to justice?'

'From my point of view,' Esther replied as her chin rose in a sign of aggression, 'I want him to answer for all those women he's frightened. But Percy and Jack want to get information from him regarding who's been paying him to do it. As you know, they suspect George Manners.'

Helen laughed lightly and shook her head.

'Believe me, George Manners wouldn't say "boo" to a goose. He's just about the wettest type of man you could imagine and the least likely to be at the head of a group of tough working types. Anyway, you may not have to place yourself in danger in order to identify Bert Freeman as the one who's been doing all these terrible things.'

'What do you mean?'

'Read this,' Helen instructed her as she lifted a letter from the pile in front of her at the kitchen table. 'It came yesterday. It's from a woman in Luton who had originally promised to recruit members in her area. She's in the catering trade herself, so she has a lot of local contacts that would have been useful to the Alliance. You may remember her name — Mabel Barker

— since she wrote in some weeks ago and cancelled her membership.'

'Only vaguely,' Esther admitted. 'But why has she written to you again?'

'Read the letter for yourself and you'll see.'

Esther frowned as she picked her way through the spidery handwriting and somewhat individualised spelling, but the sentiment was clear enough.

Dear missus Tenchart,

I'm sorri that I culdnt do what you wanted for yur union, but I were scared of a bloke what's handwritin I knew. He wus a bad basterd tu me when he lived with me, and now Iv seen the back of him I dunt want him back in mi lif.

'How could she possibly have recognised his handwriting, if it was anything like the other notes we've recovered?' Esther queried.

Helen smiled. 'If Miss Barker wrote you another letter without signing it, couldn't you identify it as coming from her simply by her own unique misuse of the English language?'

'Yes, probably, but so what?'

'According to her, she lived with the man who left her the note and could probably recognise his misspellings. Anyway, if she's right, then there's no need for you to go back into that dreadful Wapping area in the search for Bert Freeman. Mabel Barker can tell us his real name.'

'But that won't give us the man himself, will it?' Esther pointed out. 'We can go about this from two different directions. I'll find the man and you can find out his real name, in case he gives Percy the run-around.'

Helen thought for a brief moment, then nodded.

131

'I've already written to Mabel and told her that I'll be going up to Luton on the train on Saturday, since Mabel works through the week and is more likely to be at home then. You can go through with your plan with Jack and Percy and by the end of the day this entire horror story will be at an end.'

'Let's hope so. But even if we find Bert Freeman and get him locked up, I hope you'll still come and live here. This place is getting creepier by the day for me, living on my own.'

'This is Toby and Jim,' Jack advised Esther as they met up by arrangement at the bus stop outside the Alliance premises. 'Toby's the big bloke, but Jim's the best fighter. Uncle Percy's already down there, disguised as a dock worker and he'll be watching from a distance. You and I stroll around like a courting couple and Toby and Jim saunter along a few paces behind. Once you spot Freeman, let me know and I'll give the boys the signal.'

Esther felt confident enough until they alighted from the bus outside the entrance to St Katherine's Dock and walked back up in the general direction of Walpole Street. As they turned their backs on the dock gates, a scruffy looking workman with a battered and weather-beaten cap pushed himself off the wall he had been lounging against and moved slowly off fifty yards behind them. The Saturday crowds were ill-clothed and surly looking, some of them dragging protesting children behind them at a pace that was too fast for their tired legs and Esther felt completely out of place as the four of them drifted past market stalls piled high with rapidly rotting fruit, stale-looking bread and basic household items such as pots and pans.

'I hope we find him soon,' she muttered to Jack. 'I hate this place.'

'Isn't it like where you grew up?'

Esther shook her head vigorously. '*Nothing* like it. Spitalfields was genteel, in my younger days. I know you country gentry looked down on anywhere in the East End, but believe me it was nothing like this. Just imagine trying to bring up a small child on your own in a dump like this.'

'You won't have to,' Jack reminded her.

'No, thank God. But I can imagine it and I had to visit Tilly Chalmers, remember? She thinks she's so lucky, finding a man to protect her and we're about to take him off the streets.'

'Not before time. What does he look like, by the way, just to give me a general idea?'

'He's about your height, but with gingery sort of hair and one of those straggly beards that looks as if it can't make its mind up whether to grow or not. Rough looking, but curiously enough addicted to snuff, which I always took to be an upper-class thing.'

'Perhaps he's really upper-class, but enjoys slumming it.'

'I doubt that. Just along here we should reach the bottom end of Walpole Street, then we can walk up one side of it, then down the next.'

'We'll be more obvious once we get out of this crowded thoroughfare,' Jack observed, 'so let's hope he doesn't get suspicious if we do find him.'

'I sincerely hope we do,' Esther replied with a slight shudder, 'because I'd hate to have to do all this again next Saturday.'

Ten minutes later they were on their way back down Walpole Street when Esther stiffened as she saw a familiar figure amble into the street from the bottom end, towards which they were heading.

'That's him!' she whispered hoarsely to Jack. 'The one in the brown suit with the grey cap.'

Jack turned briefly to the two Yard men a few feet behind them.

'Up ahead, grey cap and brown suit, walking towards us. Sergeant Enright seems to be just ahead of him on the other side of the street.'

Their companions nodded in acknowledgement and they all kept on walking. Bert Freeman was just about to enter an alleyway a few yards away on their left when he looked up, spotted Esther and stopped dead in his tracks.

He shot into the alleyway towards which he'd been heading with all four members of Scotland Yard in hot pursuit. Up three flights of stairs at full speed, taking the steps two at a time. Jack was the quickest and kept up with Freeman's furious dash up the stairs, finally bringing him down in a crash tackle on the top landing, as he was about to unlock the door to number twelve. He lashed out with both arms and Jack went crashing against the wall just as Toby and Jim dived on top of Freeman and rolled him over, while a panting Percy Enright pulled a set of wrist restraints from his jacket and snapped them on once Toby had Freeman's arms behind his back.

'Right, Mr Freeman,' Percy announced with what little breath he had left. 'My young colleague here is going to collect a police wagon, then while the other two conduct a thorough search of this room that you conveniently identified for us, you and I are going on a little trip up to Leman Street, where I've organised another room for you. One with bars and limited cooking facilities.'

Chapter 21

'Well now, isn't this awfully cosy?' Percy gloated through the bars of the cage that kept his prisoner from carrying out the murderous attack that his eyes threatened. 'We have you booked in as "Bert Freeman", but no doubt we'll get your real name out of you in due course. Or you can save us the trouble and we could adjourn for dinner. Or at least, I could — you'll have to take yours in your room.'

'I'll kill that bitch what peached on me!' the man spat back at him.

Percy's face hardened.

'The bitch to whom I believe you're referring will be marrying my nephew in June, with me as the best man, so that was hardly a good start to our relationship, was it, Mr —?'

The man spat in Percy's direction again.

Percy sighed. 'Very well, see you in a week or two.'

Percy rose from the chair he'd drawn up in the corridor outside the open cell with bars from floor to ceiling and was five paces towards the corridor door when he was interrupted by the aggrieved voice of his prisoner.

'Yer can't hold me fer *that* long!'

'Can I not? Oh yes, how forgetful of me. You're quite right of course. Once we charge you with God knows how many offences of burglary and threats to harm innocent women, we'll be obliged by law either to release you pending trial, or hold you in custody to await that happy day. Which of those options are preferred by the magistrate will depend to a large extent on the report we give to him regarding your level of co-operation.'

'Then go ahead an' charge me!'

'I'd like nothing better, believe me, but you see there's a difficulty with that. I can't charge you until I know your real name.'

'So?'

'So you'll sit there with the smell of that pail in the corner until you tell me it. If you give us no trouble, we might even change the pail from time to time.'

''Owdyer know that Bert Freeman ain't me real name?'

'Because you're a criminal and I never knew one yet who was obliging enough to give his real name the first time around. Mind you, this might help.'

While he'd been making this last observation, the door from the corridor had opened and a uniformed turnkey had walked into the cell area carrying a large Metropolitan Police canvas holdall. He placed it on the dusty concrete floor.

'Sergeant Bradley on the front desk said ter bring this down ter yer as soon as the other bobbies brought it in, like yer asked 'im.'

'Yes, thank you,' Percy replied with a smile and the turnkey closed the door as he walked back out into the corridor. Percy untied the top of the canvas holdall and grinned.

'We brought you a change of clothing,' he advised the man behind the bars as he tipped the holdall upside down. A large collection of ladies' underwear dropped to the floor, all shapes, sizes and colours, along with several pieces of paper. Percy looked briefly at each piece, then glared up at Freeman.

'You obviously had a few messages yet to deliver. All the same, and all of them warning the intended recipient against joining a union. One has to wonder at your enthusiasm to deliver them — unless you were paid to do so, of course.'

'Yer'll get nothin' outta me!' the prisoner insisted.

Percy smiled one of his unpleasant smiles.

'That's where you're wrong, on a variety of counts. For one thing, we'll get a cheap laugh out of you when I send some of my men in here to strip all your clothes off and dress you in one of these pairs of knickers. This long-legged pink pair with the black lacework look as if they'll fit you — although I'm sure you've tried them on for size already. Then we take you back upstairs and throw you into what we call the "fish tank". That's the big holding area you were kept in when you first arrived. As you may recall, it's full of riff-raff we've pulled off the street in the past few hours. Some of them may by now be sober, but only a representative sample. Unfortunately — for you — they're a tough lot and when we throw you in there dressed in only a pair of ladies' undergarments, the reaction should be well worth watching.'

'Yer can't.'

'I can.'

'Yer wouldn't.'

'I would.'

'Whaddyer want?'

'Didn't we already discuss that? Your real name.'

'Walter Mathewson.'

'Now then, that wasn't so hard, was it?'

'An' yer won't do what yer threatened?'

'Not yet, since you've been so obliging. Now I really must be taking my leave. The pie shop across the road has my order for devilled kidney and potato — so much more filling than chicken, don't you think? I'll be back tomorrow to discuss the terms for not dressing you in those Mary-Anne knickers and throwing you to a shower of drunks, one of whom is bound to be a Nancy-boy.'

'What is it yer'll be wantin' ter know?'

'Can't you guess?'

'If I could guess, I'd be tellin' yer!'

'It's actually very simple. Who paid you to deliver all those warning notes?'

'Yer kiddin', right? Think I want ter end up face down in Katherine Dock wi' me arms an' legs tied tergevver, an' a brick in me trousers?'

'I certainly wouldn't welcome that personally, so I see your point. But you added your own personal blessing to some of them, didn't you? Why *was* that, exactly?'

'Them was the ones they wanted *really* scared shitless.'

'But the sexual flavour of those pencilled additions was just your idea of fun, was it? That wasn't suggested to you by whoever was paying you?'

'No, they was my idea. Give me quite a stiffy, doin' that.'

'I'll leave you for the day, Mr Mathewson, partly because it's my dinner time and partly because the urge to take my billy club and batter your privates flat is becoming almost irresistible. Sleep tight and I hope the bugs bite.'

Back upstairs, he gave instructions that Mathewson was to be held in custody until further notice, then wandered out into the still busy street and lit his pipe. As he looked up, he found himself staring at a couple sitting at a table on the pavement outside the chop house that he had favoured when attached to Leman Street Police Station during the Ripper investigations coming up for two years ago. His brain was so preoccupied with working out the best strategy for getting Mathewson to divulge the identity of his paymasters that it took him a second or two to recognise Jack and Esther. He walked over to their table.

'Let me buy you one of your favourite chicken pies and a mug of tea,' Jack offered as he rose from his seat.

Percy nodded as he looked down at Esther.

'Thank you *so* much for your assistance today. You must be very relieved that it's all over.'

'But it's not really, is it?' Esther replied with a penetrating stare into his eyes. 'We've got the monkey, but not the organ grinder. Did Freeman tell you anything valuable?'

'Only his real name, or at least what he claims is his real name. Walter Mathewson, according to him. You got the Wally right, anyway.'

'How long will he go away for?'

'Assuming he's found guilty, I'll be pushing for ten years minimum.'

'Do you get a say in it?'

'No, of course not, but I can lean on the prosecuting counsel to argue long and hard with the judge.'

'Here you go, Uncle,' Jack enthused as he returned, carefully carrying a chicken pie in a paper bag and a large mug stained slightly on the outside with the tea of ages past. 'I take it that Esther and Helen will now be no longer at risk?'

'Not from Mathewson, anyway. But now we have to find the person who employed him. Your first job tomorrow, Jack, is to get back into records and see if Mathewson has any known associates.'

'At least we won't have to go to Barking, even though it's Sunday tomorrow,' Esther added. 'Your "seven on, two off" shifts are very convenient from that point of view and I can spend tomorrow clearing my room ahead of Helen moving in. She's gone up to Luton today, to speak to a woman who claims she knows the man you've identified as Mathewson. She doesn't know yet that you've caught him, obviously, but I kept my part of the deal with her.'

'What deal was that, exactly?' Percy enquired.

'I was to help you catch Mathewson — or "Freeman" as we knew him then — and she was to get evidence that he was the man responsible for all the break-ins. I can't wait for her come back on Monday and give me all her news. Will you two want to come over to talk to her?'

'I'll be over, certainly,' Jack said. 'This latest enquiry has given me perfect excuses for being with you during the working day.'

'Don't forget to pull Mathewson's record before you do that,' Percy reminded him. 'I'll probably be at the Yard all day, following up any criminal connections between our man and those likely to have been employing him. Like you, I have an excuse for not being in Barking, although that does mean my continued exposure to yet another of your aunt's culinary failures. She's the only woman I know who can burn gravy.'

Esther giggled.

'I'm sure it's not that bad and I for one welcome any freedom from constant enquiries regarding the wedding preparations and persistent reminders regarding my residential obligation.'

'At the risk of sounding like my sister-in-law, how exactly *are* preparations going?' Percy enquired as he took the last mouthful of chicken pie.

'Pretty well, on the whole,' Jack replied, but Esther wasn't letting him off so easily.

'What Jack means is that my wedding dress is almost complete, which is of course the only part of the "preparations" that I have control over. As for the decoration of our new residence, Jack has continued to demonstrate the wisdom of his choice of career in the police force, rather than any ambition he might have entertained to be a decorator.'

'It wasn't my fault if the wallpaper didn't want to stay on the wall,' Jack protested.

'It's all a matter of the consistency of the paste you apply,' Percy advised him. 'I've done enough wallpapering over the years to know that you have to apply the paste thickly, then let it sort of congeal for a minute or two before applying it to the wall.'

'But it smells so disgusting while it's sitting there,' Esther complained, 'so it might be my fault for insisting that Jack put the paper on the wall too early. What's in that awful paste, anyway?'

'Arsenic, for one thing,' Percy explained. 'Most manufacturers include it as a deterrent to bugs. But it's also in a lot of wallpapers, from which it's released into the room when it gets moist on the underside. Have you by any chance chosen a paper that's heavily green in colour?'

Esther and Jack exchanged guilty glances and Esther nodded.

'Yes. I really liked the one that had trees and lawns, with deer roaming around and squirrels bounding through the grass.'

'It's also a real bugger to match the pattern up at the seams,' Jack complained.

'Take my advice,' Percy warned them, 'and leave doors and windows open while you're putting the paper up. Use as little paste as you can get away with — but more than you're using at present, by the sound of things — and whack it on the wall without waiting too long. And watch out for the symptoms of arsenic poisoning.'

'What are they?' Esther enquired fearfully.

'Sore throat, breathing difficulties, stomach cramps, headaches, light-headedness, and — in some cases — hallucinations.'

'Horrible!' Esther grimaced. 'Perhaps we should change our wallpaper — we've almost run out anyway, thanks to Jack's incompetence.'

'I warned you that the pattern was difficult to match up at the seams,' Jack protested, then turned to look at Percy. 'If we strip off the stuff we've already put on the walls, will that remove the danger?'

'Yes, once it's off. But depending upon how you strip it, you'll be exposing yourself to even more arsenic. Put a cloth or handkerchief over your face while you're about it. Does your new house have a common garden area at the back?' Percy enquired.

Jack nodded.

'Then take the paper you pull from the wall in a bag down into the garden and burn it,' Percy advised him. 'And now it's time we got back to work. Jack can go back to the Yard and extract Mr Mathewson's no doubt extensive criminal history, while I'll take myself back down to his room in Wapping, to see if the searches down there have yielded any skeleton keys. At least we know of one door we can try them on.'

'If you mean Helen Trenchard's front door, I'm coming with you,' Jack insisted. 'You two were getting far too friendly over dinner last Saturday.'

'I can't help it if I've retained some of my natural charm over the years,' Percy grinned, 'although Mr Mathewson wasn't blessed with any of it during my conversation with him over the road there.'

'He gave you no clue as to who his criminal associates might have been?' Jack enquired.

Percy shook his head. 'Not yet, but he will.'

Esther turned back to wave to Jack as the omnibus pulled away from its stop, then extracted the keys from her handbag and made her way towards the front door of her temporary residence, her mind still absorbing the implications of Percy's warnings regarding the wallpapering and frustrated by the prospect of more delay while Jack's first efforts were removed from the wall and burned in the rear garden. Then they'd have to choose new wallpaper and start all over again.

She subconsciously noted the sound of someone inside working on a sewing machine, before snapping to attention with the realisation that there'd been no sewing machine in there since Isaac had used one for sewing pockets into men's suits. As she quickly opened the front door and stepped inside, the noise stopped abruptly and she put it down to her tired brain and the likelihood that the noise had been coming from somewhere in the street behind her. After a brief supper of leftover soup and slightly stale bread, she crept up to bed, relieved that the capture of Bert Freeman was over without anyone being seriously injured.

She woke up with the Sunday morning sun streaming through her window and the happy thought that today she could put the finishing touches to her wedding dress, which was hanging proudly on a hook on the bedroom wall. After breakfasting on the last of the bread, smeared with honey, she carefully washed her hands and carried the dress downstairs into her 'office', happily reminding herself that the Alliance would probably soon grow rapidly again, now that the man scaring member's off was safely behind bars.

She hummed quietly to herself as she sewed imitation flowers into the white lace overlay that she'd already painstakingly sewn onto the basic white dress cut from the pattern, then realised that she was humming out of tune with the faint melody that she could hear through the wall behind her. Not just out of tune, but a different tune altogether. She put down her intricate sewing and listened more carefully, then shivered when she realised what she was hearing.

It was an old Hebrew folk tune that had grown familiar to her two years previously, when Isaac had hummed it in his curious high-pitched way that was totally unlike his normal speaking voice. And now it seemed that Isaac was humming it again, from the space behind her office wall that had once been his curtained off portion of the old workplace. But Isaac had been dead for eighteen months or so.

Curious, but shivering with anticipation, she slipped out of her office space, through the soon to be outer office area and round to the back, where Isaac's previous workspace was now serving as a storage area. As she peered, trembling, into the open and empty area, the sound of humming stopped dead and she shook her head to clear her ears. Then she walked to the window that looked out over Lamb Street for some simple explanation of what she'd heard earlier.

Or perhaps only *thought* she'd heard. What had Percy warned them about hallucinations as a symptom of arsenic poisoning? And if she was suffering these hopefully minor symptoms, what must Jack be suffering, since he'd been exposed to the wallpaper and paste more than she had? She was looking forward even more to Jack's promised arrival the following day when she could ask him. And of course, Helen would be back tomorrow and the place wouldn't be so empty, and somehow eerie, with the growing feeling that someone was watching her every move.

Esther's excited anticipation of Helen's return to work proved unjustified when Helen failed to appear at all on the Monday. When Jack knocked on the front door at around dinner time, bearing two portions of lamb wrapped tightly inside fresh crusty bread, she voiced her concerns as she put the pan on to boil for tea.

'She probably took today off in lieu of Saturday,' Jack suggested. 'Where was she going, again?'

'Luton, or so she said,' Esther replied. 'We got a letter from a former member of the Alliance who claimed that the man calling himself Bert Freeman was known to her. Helen was intending to go up there and chat with her and I was looking forward to advising her that we'd caught him and that he'd given us his real name.'

'I don't think he did,' Jack replied gloomily.

Esther looked across the table at him with raised eyebrows as she bit into her dinner.

'I've spent nearly two days examining Criminal Records for a Walter Mathewson,' Jack explained. 'I found three and the worst that they could come up with between them recently was a "drunk and insensible" in Bishopsgate, although one of them had a bit of form for burglary and indecent assault. However, that was as a juvenile and was a few years in the past. If your Mr Freeman gave his correct name, then he's managed to keep his nose clean with the Met for an amazing number of years for a man of his habits.'

'*Please* don't call him "my" Mr Freeman,' Esther protested through a mouthful of bread and roast lamb. 'Surely it doesn't matter what the dreadful man's name is, since you've got him behind bars?'

'It does if we want to find the people behind his actions,' Jack reminded her. 'Uncle Percy's not at all happy that I couldn't find him and is now busy using the Yard's extensive telephone network to see if they've heard of him in Essex, Middlesex, Surrey, or anywhere else just outside the Met. He thinks Mathewson may be a blow-in from the outer suburbs hoping to lose himself in the big bad city.'

'Has he tried Bedfordshire?' Esther enquired.

'No idea, why?'

Esther tutted. 'I *really* do make a better detective than you sometimes. Where's Luton situated?'

'Oh, I see,' Jack admitted reluctantly. 'I'll suggest that to him.'

'And pretend that it was your idea?' Esther challenged him. 'While we're on the subject of your failings, when can we go and choose some more wallpaper? I'd be glad to get out of here for a while. It's getting a bit creepy, rattling around here on my own. I've started imagining things, which may be a symptom of that wallpaper disease that your uncle took great delight in telling us about.'

'What sorts of things?'

'Never mind. Let's finish our dinner and go shopping. I'll leave a note for Helen.'

By Wednesday there was still no sign of Helen and Esther was becoming seriously concerned. Jack had taken to joining her for dinner every day, a process he justified as 'pursuing enquiries' regarding the burglaries that Mathewson, or whoever he was, had been carrying out. By Wednesday he was prepared to agree with Esther that something was seriously wrong and with a reminder that he'd be resuming wallpaper duties the following day he set off after a lingering kiss.

When the knock came on the door well after dark that same evening, Esther was preparing herself to reluctantly order him off the doorstep. But this time he'd come armed with his uncle and both of them looked as if they'd lost a pound and found a penny.

'Can we come in?' Percy enquired solicitously.

'Of course,' Esther replied as she opened the door wider to admit both men. As they stood there in the front foyer, Percy nodded to the chair that sat behind the intended reception area desk.

'Best sit on that, my dear.'

'Why?'

'Because I don't want you falling over and damaging anything. Either of yours or the Alliance's.'

'There's only the counter,' Esther pointed out, 'and I could easily explain that to Helen, when she finally gets round to coming back to work.'

Percy remained ominously silent as Jack took Esther's arm and guided her into the chair.

'She won't be coming back, I'm afraid,' Percy explained.

Esther's hand flew to her mouth.

'What's happened to her?'

'She was found dead in a laneway in Luton,' Jack advised her gently. 'Murdered, so it would seem.'

Chapter 22

'How did you find out?' Esther whispered, ashen-faced.

'Depressingly easily,' Percy told her. 'When Jack advised me of where Helen had gone on Saturday, in response to a letter from someone who knew Mathewson, as he's now confirmed to be, I made a telephone call to the police at Luton, which is a very small, self-contained, borough force that knew Wally Mathewson only too well and were delighted when he decided not to return into their midst after his most recent stretch for theft and indecent assault. He was, apparently, a menace to young girls in Bedfordshire generally and Luton in particular.'

'Esther wants to know about Helen, Uncle,' Jack reminded him.

'Yes, sorry. I asked if they knew anyone in Luton who we could contact to get more information about him and they gave us the name of a woman...'

'Mabel Barker,' Esther announced in a flat tone that was indicative of shock. 'She was the woman that Helen set out to visit.'

'Indeed, and she may be able to confirm everything else we know.'

'*You* may know, but Esther doesn't,' Jack prompted him grumpily.

Percy continued: 'The person I was speaking to gave me the address and added, quite coincidentally, that he'd been to that street only three days before, to a woman's body that had been found only a few yards down from Mabel Barker's house. I asked if it was Mabel herself and he replied that it was believed to be a woman called Helen Trenchard, according to a clothing name label found on the body. I told him that I knew a woman of that name, in connection with certain enquiries involving Wally Mathewson and we agreed that everything seemed to fit together. To cut a long story short, Jack and I will be travelling to Luton tomorrow to perform the formal identification and to question Mabel Barker regarding what might have got Helen murdered. The chances are that she was given certain information that someone didn't want to have revealed and that may well lead us to the person who was pulling Mathewson's strings.'

'Do you want me to come with you?' Esther said without any audible enthusiasm.

Percy shook his head. 'Best that you stay here and recover from the shock. In addition, I imagine that there are certain arrangements you'll have to make regarding the Alliance.'

Esther raised her eyes with a blank look.

'The Alliance presumably died when Helen did. I can hang around here for a while, tidying up loose ends, but I can only assume that I'm out of a job. I'll be making an earlier transfer to Barking than I'd expected, no doubt to Constance Enright's considerable satisfaction.'

'Mother will be delighted to look after you, I'm sure,' Jack reassured her, 'but you can see why I have to put the wallpapering on hold.'

'If you show me how to do it, I can probably have it done in half the time, given that I'm unemployed all of a sudden.' Esther managed to smile. 'And it might even stay on the wall when I do it.'

'You'll probably feel at a loose end tomorrow,' Percy observed, 'so why not take yourself over to Lucy's?'

'I might, since you suggest it.' Esther nodded. 'But when will you be able to take your next days off, Jack?'

'Not until this is over, probably,' Jack replied, 'but I'll say what Uncle Percy was too tactful to say. If Helen murdered for reasons connected with the Alliance and you remain living here, still working for the Alliance, you're making yourself the next likely victim.'

'I need to be getting home,' Percy announced as he glanced at his fob watch, then at Jack. 'We have an early start in the morning. I'll meet you at St Pancras at eight am.' He looked across at Esther. 'I'll leave you in the capable hands of my nephew here.'

As the front door closed behind him, Esther rose from her chair on slightly wobbly legs and Jack took her arm.

'Let me help you upstairs,' he offered.

Esther smiled. 'Nice try. When your uncle announced that he was leaving me in the capable hands of his nephew, he had no idea of what his nephew's hands were capable *of.* I'll see myself to bed, thank you all the same.'

'Spoilsport,' Jack muttered as he kissed her warmly on the lips.

'That's definitely Helen Trenchard,' Percy confirmed the following morning, as he looked down at the body on the mortuary table. Jack looked the other way.

'Manual strangulation,' the pathologist advised him as he pointed to the blackened area around the throat that had been surgically incised. 'Fractured hyoid bone. A dead giveaway.'

'Unfortunate use of words,' Percy replied laconically. 'May we see the possessions?'

'On the table over there,' the pathologist said, nodding to it. Percy and Jack walked across the room to examine them.

'Take a look in this handbag. What do you deduce?' Percy asked Jack.

'Robbery,' Jack replied enthusiastically. 'There's no purse.'

'Good. Now what else?'

'Nothing. There's nothing in the handbag.'

'Precisely. Yet we're advised that Miss Trenchard was a keen unionist who was visiting a former member who could give her information about Mathewson. If you'd set out on a mission like that, would you not have taken at least a notebook and pencil?'

'Yes, but I'm a police officer.'

'And a very unobservant one. How did she get here?'

'By train — at least, that was her intention.'

'Precisely. Do you see the return half of her ticket?'

'Perhaps she bought a single.'

'And perhaps I'll be the next Pope. Assuming that she bought a return, why did her murderer take the return half?'

'To use it himself?'

'Or perhaps to conceal where the victim had come from.'

'A lot of people use St Pancras, Uncle. How could anyone possibly have identified her from her possession of a ticket to St Pancras?'

'When they got around to interviewing locals, would Mabel Barker have not told them that she'd had a visit the same day from a woman who came from London? The next logical question for the local police is to ask *why* someone had come from London all the way into darkest Bedfordshire in order to speak to a waitress in the local cattle market boardroom. A finger then points to the Alliance and enquiries at the Alliance point to Wally Mathewson, who just happened to know Mabel Barker. Someone was covering their tracks.'

Esther sat, utterly despondent, on the lowest stair, with her head cupped in her hands and her elbows balanced on her knees. She stared blankly out at the alterations that had so recently been made to the inside of what she best remembered as a bespoke tailor's business and caught herself wishing that it still was, until she reminded herself that those were the days before she met Jack. She wondered how they were getting on in Luton and wished that Jack was there beside her. Not to give her any practical advice — he was useless at anything like that — but to make her feel wanted and valued, with a purpose in life that made it worth the effort of living it.

Somehow she had to honour Helen's memory by ensuring that the Alliance closed down with dignity and with its books in proper order. She had been trusted enough to be given operational access to the account with the local bank, so she knew that there was enough in there to keep paying her wages of ten shillings a week. This had been almost an irrelevance from the start, given her independent wealth at that time, but following the purchase of the Clerkenwell rooms and other expenses including decorating materials, it might become important in the future.

She'd never been in the job for the money though; it had been more a matter of pride and an excuse not to fall into the fulltime clutches of Constance Enright. The way Esther felt every time that she and Jack made bodily contact left her in no doubt that she'd be a mother well before the June of the following year and she'd been hoping to prove her value as a working woman before being thrown onto the same childbirth roundabout as every other married woman — and many unmarried ones — with the reduced status that society afforded all mothers, as if rearing the next generation wasn't the most important work in human society.

Thoughts about her forthcoming marriage reminded her that she was obliged by law to live in Barking for the entire month before the proclaiming of the 'banns' in the local parish church, according to that odious vicar. Since those banns had to be proclaimed for three consecutive weeks after that, Esther was committed to a seven week sojourn in Barking that felt like an impending prison sentence. The least she could do, in her own defence, was to ensure that it was no longer than that.

A quick perusal of the lease that Helen had taken over the Lamb Street premises disclosed that it was for a year, with the first six months of rent payable in advance in two instalments and the second full instalment payable at least a month prior to the expiry of those six months. A quick sum on a piece of paper had revealed that the half-yearly rent was due at the end of March, a month short of the date when Esther would be obliged to reside temporarily in Barking. She had no doubt that Constance would gleefully allow her to move in at the end of March, but Esther had in mind keeping the bank account going with sufficient funds in it to pay the next rental instalment. However, she also had an uncomfortable feeling that this might be dishonest. Membership subscriptions were still coming in, and increasingly so in recent weeks, but they were from unsuspecting working women who believed that they were thereby obtaining the protection and support of an ongoing viable union, not an organisation that had lost its founder and only driving force.

This also of course necessitated, if only morally, that existing members be advised that the Alliance had ceased to be and that hopeful applicants be advised that there was no longer anything to join. The first thing she should do — and it would occupy days of her time — was to write to every existing member, advising them of Helen's death and enquiring if any of them might be interested in continuing with the great work that Helen had started. She would also need to reply to everyone who wrote seeking membership. She had checked the notepaper supply that Helen had stacked in the storage area to the rear and there was probably enough to complete the mammoth task. There was also probably enough ink and Esther had her own supply of nibbed pens. The only possible flaw in her plan was that her own writing hand might give up the ghost before the mountain she was confronting could be climbed.

She sighed, went upstairs for a cup of tea and sent a silent prayer to Isaac, the man who had never accepted defeat, even in his darkest days.

'The chances are that Mabel Barker doesn't know that Helen's dead,' Percy advised Jack as they plodded up Station Road towards the address that the local police had supplied, 'and if she finds out, she'll probably clam up on us. After all, it looks as if Helen may have been killed on the mere suspicion that Mabel had told her something really important regarding the identity of the person behind the sabotage of the Alliance, and Mabel may form the not unreasonable fear that she'll be next if she gives us that same information.'

'But how can we ask the questions of her without revealing why we're here?' Jack

Percy smiled and tapped his nose.

'Lots of women in London have been the victims of intimidating behaviour by Mathewson, have they not? Mabel wrote and told Helen that she knew who was behind the attack on her and we simply tell her that we're after further evidence to put Mathewson away for a long time. Once she knows that he's safely locked up, she may be more forthcoming. I'll ask the questions and you just sit there and take notes, agreed?'

'Agreed.'

The door was opened to them by a lady who was probably no older than thirty and whose active occupation had kept her slim enough. But the wispy, almost straw-like auburn hair with grey streaks that poked out from under her working cap and the deepening lines beneath her eyes, revealed Mabel Barker to be a woman who was about to descend into the early middle age that seemed to be the fate of all women who earned their own living in a man's world. There was no sign of any children, so Mabel had probably opted to do so alone.

Percy raised his police badge high in the air and smiled.

'Detective Sergeant Enright, Mrs Barker. This gentlemen and I are from Scotland Yard.

'*Miss* Barker, but come in,' she said resignedly as she opened the door wider. 'Take a seat in the parlour there; I were gonna make a cup o' tea anyway. It's about Wally Mathewson, ain't it?'

'I take it that Miss Trenchard has been in touch?' Percy enquired tactfully.

'Yeah, she come last Sat'day an' I don't think I can tell you any more than I told 'er, ter be 'onest wi' yer.'

Percy smiled encouragingly.

'It was Miss Trenchard who suggested that we come and talk to you, Miss Barker. First of all, let me reassure you that we have Mr Mathewson safely locked up in the police cells in Whitechapel, so you have nothing to fear from telling us whatever you can about him, and the people he associated with.'

'If yer've got 'im locked up, why d'yer need any more from me? 'E's bin at it agin, down in London, ain't 'e?'

'At what, exactly?' Percy asked.

Mabel's face screwed up in a gesture of disgust.

'Stealin' ladies' unmentionables. Off washin' lines, like mine, or else out of their 'ouses. Sometimes off young girls an' all — while they was still wearin' 'em.'

'Yes, I'm afraid he has,' Percy conceded. 'But he's also taken to frightening his victims by leaving them notes suggesting that he'll return and do nasty things to them.'

'That's what 'e did ter me an' all,' Mabel grimaced. 'D'yer wanna see the note?'

'Yes please, that would be very helpful.' Percy smiled and Mabel went to a cupboard on the far side of the room, which she opened to reveal a quantity of crockery neatly arranged on wooden shelves. From a cutlery drawer she extracted a sheet of paper, unfolded it and handed it to Percy, who read it and frowned.

'He was threatening to come back for you?'

'Yeah, like it says. I were wi' 'im afore, yer see an' when 'e come outer Bedford Gaol the last time, 'e wanted me ter go wi' 'im down ter London, but I said no.'

'You're sure this is his handwriting?'

'Dead right I'm sure. 'E used ter write me little love notes when we first met.'

'How did you first meet?'

'It were when I were first workin' at the cattle yards an' 'e were called in ter put up some fences. 'E's a woodworker by trade, yer see, an' 'im an' me got talkin' an' larkin' about, yer know the way it is? Then 'e started leavin' me little notes an' one thing led ter anovver an' then there we was, livin' tergevver.'

'How long did that last?'

'A coupla years, then one day the bobbies come an' accused 'im o' stealin' some underwear from a woman down the road. It were very embarrassin', as yer can imagine, but 'e promised me it wouldn't 'appen again an' I were stupid enough ter believe 'im. When it 'appened again, an' this time 'e pushed this young girl inter a ditch an' took off 'er undies, well that were it. I threw 'im out, but 'e kept comin' back an' askin' me to forgive 'im. But I couldn't take the worry o' wonderin' when it'd 'appen again an' all the embarrassment an' that, so I kept sayin' no. But 'e could get violent an' all, so I were very relieved when 'e finally got that three year stretch an' I thought that were the end've it.'

'But he came back when he was released from prison?'

'Yeah, that were the last time I seen 'im. Musta bin three months or more now an' I come 'ome from work an' there 'e was, sittin' in me little laundry place, out the back there, shelterin' from the rain. 'E said as 'ow while 'e were in prison, this couple 'ad bin ter see 'im an' offered 'im a job in London. 'E said it were regular work an' we could set up again tergevver down there, but I told 'im ter sling 'is 'ook. The next thing I knew were that note pinned ter me washin' line an' a pair o' me knickers gone.'

'Did he by any chance say anything more about this man and woman who visited him in prison?' Percy enquired, as Jack wrote furiously in his notebook.

'Not really, just that it were a Nancy lookin' bloke wi' an older woman an' that they was settin' up some sorta woodworkin' organisation down the East End. Wappin', I think it were, but I could be wrong.'

'Just one final thing, Miss Barker.' Percy smiled again. 'Did Mathewson have any irritating personal habits?'

'Like what?'

157

'Well, was he a heavy smoker, or did he perhaps bite his nails or something?'

'Yer mean the snuff, don't yer?'

'He took snuff?'

'All the bloody time. The filthy stuff got on me clothes, me table cloths, even me bed sheets some times.'

'Thank you, Miss Barker, that's helped us tremendously,' Percy assured her as he rose to leave, and Jack followed suit after closing his notebook. As they reached the front door and were turning for one final farewell, Mabel grabbed Percy's arm.

'There were a woman murdered down the road there Sat'day night. Were that ... you know, whatsername?'

'I was only here to ask you about Wally Mathewson, Miss Barker. The local police can give you any other information you need. You might want to talk to them, but rest assured that Wally's safely locked away where you'll never see him again.'

'Is it good police practice to lie to witnesses?' Jack said accusingly as they walked back towards the station.

'I didn't lie,' Percy argued. 'I just didn't tell her the entire truth. It *is* good practice not to leave them scared witless.'

'The only one she should be scared of is Mathewson and we know it can't have been him who murdered Helen, so who *was* it?'

'That's a question to which we currently have no answer. But I suggest that first thing tomorrow morning we pay a visit to the lady in Lambeth who reported Helen's murder to the police, and I'd bet money that it turns out to be a false address. That will be good in one sense, but not in another.'

'How could it possibly be good?' Jack enquired, genuinely puzzled.

'Because it will all but confirm that whoever that woman was, she was the one who murdered Helen Trenchard. My real problem at the moment is working out how she knew that Helen was visiting Mabel Barker.'

It fell silent for a long time, but by the time they reached the ticket barrier, Jack had to ask, if only for his own peace of mind, 'You surely don't suspect Esther, do you?'

'Of course not. Is that why you've been uncharacteristically silent for the past few minutes? I thought it might be something else.'

'Such as?'

'I hate to be the one to bring it to your attention, but someone knew that Helen was planning to visit Mabel Barker. Apart from Esther, there's no-one working inside the Alliance office. So that raises the very worrying thought that someone's been listening in to conversations there.'

'How?'

'I don't know yet, obviously. But after we visit Lambeth tomorrow morning, we'll be paying your fiancée a visit.'

Esther opened the door with a big smile, which faded instantly when she saw the looks on their faces.

'Not good news, obviously,' she observed. 'Come in and have a cup of tea.'

'We confirmed that the man preying on all your members was almost certainly Wally Mathewson,' Percy advised her as he selected a ginger biscuit and appeared to be interrogating it, 'and that's the good news.'

'But you've got him locked up, so what's bad about that?' Esther asked with what she hoped was an encouraging smile.

'It obviously wasn't Mathewson who murdered Helen,' Percy reminded her, 'so we were correct in suspecting that he was acting in league with others and the finger still points at that rival union. Someone connected with them must have sent someone after Helen and we don't know who that was. However, the chances are that it was a woman. It was a woman who reported finding the body and the address she gave in Lambeth turned out to be a tanner's yard.'

'So what can you do next?'

Percy looked Esther directly in the eye.

'Forgive me, but I have to ask this. You told nobody else that Helen was taking the train up to Luton last Saturday?'

'Of course not, why should I? Perhaps Helen did, but I certainly didn't.'

'When did she make that decision, can you remember?'

Esther gazed unseeingly at the far wall as she tried to recall recent events.

'I think it was on the Monday before she went up there. We got the letter from Mabel Barker on the Monday and Helen wrote back immediately to advise her of her intention to call on her on the Saturday. Then of course she had to rearrange the landlord's inspection, because she didn't want me to be here alone when they did it.' She paused briefly, then her jaw dropped. 'Oh, dear God!' she whispered.

'Let me guess,' Percy said grimly. 'She called in at the landlords to cancel the Saturday inspection because she had another matter to attend to on that day?'

'She went to see the landlords, certainly, but obviously I don't know what she said to them. And why would she need to give them that much detail?'

'Did the inspection occur on another day?'

'Yes, the day before — that would have been the Friday. It had to be that week, according to the landlords, because the first three month period was up and the terms of the lease required an inspection of any alterations that we'd carried out during that period. As you can see downstairs, they were substantial.'

'Who actually carried out the inspection?'

'Mr Bowden, from the property firm. He's the man in charge of leases, apparently.'

'Anyone else?'

'I've no idea, since I was out doing some shopping. When I got back, Helen told me that Bowden had been and gone.'

'Did Helen remain with him all the time during the inspection, do you know?' Percy queried.

'I don't know,' Esther replied. 'Helen preferred to work up here in the kitchen, so I imagine that she just left him to wander around the place.'

'Where do you keep your correspondence?' Percy asked as he selected his third ginger biscuit.

'Everywhere,' Esther replied, her hands outstretched to indicate the extent of 'everywhere'. 'If the letters needed to be answered, they'd remain here in the kitchen until Helen had done that. Then the original letter would go downstairs into my office for filing and quite frankly it's a bit of a mess down there at the moment. I'm in the process of writing to all members and potential members to advise them of Helen's death.'

'But,' Percy thought out loud as he followed what she was telling them, 'if Helen got the letter from Mabel Barker on the Monday and replied to it the same day, or even the day after, the original letter from Mabel would be lying somewhere in your office on the Friday — the day of the inspection — where it could be seen by this Bowden bloke and read, while he was hidden from sight inside your office, and Helen was here in the kitchen?'

'Yes, I suppose so,' Esther conceded, 'but he wouldn't have seen Helen's reply, would he?'

'Follow my line of reasoning,' Percy requested. 'Helen goes into the offices of Hemmingsworth and advises them that she has an appointment somewhere on the Saturday. Even if she didn't tell them precisely where, they knew that she would be somewhere on the Saturday, away from the office. On the day before that, Bowden comes in here, on the pretence of conducting an inspection, but looking for some clue as to where Helen might be heading. He reads Mabel's letter, which tells him that Mabel can identify the man who's been scaring off all your members. It also gives him a strong clue as to where Helen might be going on the Saturday, and he — or somebody — follows her. They wait until she's on her way back to the station, probably in the dark, and do the deed.'

'But why would Bowden, and for that matter the company he works for, want Helen not to find out what Mabel could tell her?'

'I didn't tell you all that we learned from Mabel,' Percy advised her. 'It seems that Mathewson was visited in prison by somebody offering him a job in London with some sort of woodworking association. Mabel didn't call it a union, because presumably Mathewson didn't tell her that and possibly didn't know anyway. All he *did* tell her was that he'd been visited by what she called "a Nancy looking bloke".'

'Helen told me all about that union!' Esther proclaimed excitedly. 'It was run by an admirer of hers who gave her advice when she was setting up the Alliance. She wasn't keen on him, because apparently he was a bit effeminate and prone to wearing perfume, but it was some sort of woodworker's union. I think I can find the name for you, if you give me a while.'

Percy smiled triumphantly, opened his notebook, flipped it back a few pages, and announced, '"The Union of Allied Woodworkers and Turners", General Secretary a Mr George Manners.'

'That sounds like the man Helen was telling me about,' Esther confirmed. 'But how does he tie in, if at all, with Hemmingsworths?'

'His union is a major shareholder in Hemmingsworths.'

'So you're suggesting that it was someone from Hemmingsworths who killed Helen?' Jack interrupted, thoroughly confused.

'Hemmingsworths, or someone hired by Hemmingsworths, like they perhaps hired Mathewson.'

Esther grimaced, then shivered. 'But would Mabel Barker's knowledge of the link between Mathewson and the union be enough to kill Helen for?'

'And for that matter,' Jack chimed in, 'how was the union, or Hemmingsworths if we add them to the suspect list, to know that Mathewson wouldn't reveal that link anyway, when you had him down in the cells?'

Percy smiled grimly.

'Mathewson made it very clear to me, during our very unpleasant, but brief, conversation, that he was more scared of whoever gave him his orders than he was of anything I could threaten him with.'

'There's still something missing in all this,' Jack objected after further thought. 'If we assume that Helen didn't reveal to anyone at Hemmingsworths that Mabel could tell her something important — and why would she? — why did they find it necessary to follow her up there and silence her? Is it not possible that it was Helen herself who was the real target?'

'For her rejected suitor?' Percy enquired with a sceptical raised eyebrow. 'And if she was the real target, why follow her all the way to Luton? Why not just lie in wait for her in a dark street here in London, or simply break into her house? Mathewson had a spare key, remember?'

'He did until we took it off him,' Jack reminded him. 'By Saturday, he was in Whitechapel Gaol.'

'But *before* Saturday?' Percy reminded him. 'The plan to follow Helen was devised before Saturday, obviously, so if whoever murdered her just wanted her dead, why not send in Mathewson earlier, making use of his spare key?'

'I'm confused,' Jack admitted dejectedly.

'And I'm frightened,' Esther added. 'If Hemmingsworths are behind this, they have a spare key to this place.'

'Didn't those locksmiths come round as instructed, to fit new ones?' Percy enquired.

Esther nodded. 'They did, but in accordance with the terms of the lease, we gave a set of the new keys to Hemmingsworths. Fortunately Helen left the main set with me, since I live here at present, but if Hemmingsworths really are involved in all this, then they can still get in at all hours of day or night.'

'Time you went to stay with Lucy,' Jack insisted. 'At least until we can establish whether the link lies with Hemmingsworths or this union.'

'Any ideas?' Percy asked.

Esther nodded again. 'I'll probably regret saying this the minute the two of you are out of the door down there, but I'm now officially unemployed, correct?'

'Yes, but so what?' Jack enquired. 'When I get to take those days off I'm due, we can get back to the wallpapering.'

Percy looked meaningfully at Esther and smiled. 'The union?'

'The union,' Esther replied with a nod to reinforce her words. 'They may just be interested in employing a young lady with recent union clerical experience.'

'No!' Jack said firmly.

Esther looked round at him defiantly as she removed her hand from his. '"No" to the idea that the union may be looking for an experienced employee? Or "no" to the suggestion that I do it? Am I being undervalued as a mere female yet again?'

'No,' Jack replied uncertainly. 'It's just ... well ... yes, I don't want you exposed to any danger.'

'And I'm sick to my back teeth of sitting here writing one identical letter after another,' Esther insisted. 'It's either wallpapering or I go down to the union and ask for a job.'

'We can get back to the wallpapering on Wednesday,' Jack promised.

'Good,' Esther replied with sickly-sweet sarcasm, 'then I can go job-hunting tomorrow.'

'You're one Hell of a lady,' Percy whispered admiringly as he kissed her on the cheek in the front doorway in the half light and nodded back inside. 'Just don't let Jack talk you out of it.'

Chapter 23

Esther tried to ignore the fact that she was back in Wapping, that dreadful collection of slums on the north bank of the Thames where she'd met Tilly Chalmers, bumped into Wally Mathewson, then assisted in his arrest a week later. This time she was standing halfway down Cable Street, outside the front door of the Union of Allied Woodworkers and Turners, twisting the handles of her handbag nervously and wondering what on earth had possessed her to volunteer for this. But her pride wouldn't let her back out now, so she pushed open the front door and walked briskly in as if she had a legitimate reason for being a mere woman in what was presumably a male domain.

There was a moderately sized open area, on the far side of which was a counter of some sort that appeared to be unattended. Around the walls were various notices relating to the union that occupied the ground floor, along with various others that appeared to be copies of newspaper articles about unions that had been photographed, then 'blown up', as the expression went, to a larger and readable size for anyone standing in front of them and looking up.

Esther was in the process of looking for some sort of bell on the front counter when a door opened behind it and a rough looking workman walked out of an office behind the rear wall. He seemed slightly taken aback when he saw Esther there in all her finery and after looking her up and down for a moment in a manner that made her feel distinctly uncomfortable, he was the first to speak.

'Can I 'elp yer, Miss?'

'I'm looking for a Mr George Manners.'

'In there.' The man gestured with his head to the office he had just come out of, then walked from behind the counter and made his way back out into Cable Street. Esther walked round to the door in question and knocked twice, only hearing the somewhat feeble response on the second occasion. With an increasing heart beat she pulled on the doorhandle and walked in.

The smell of cheap pomade hit her almost like a smack in the face. She recognised it from her days in Spitalfields, when the men who lived in the same lodging house as her would drown themselves in it, in the belief that it somehow eliminated their other body odours. It had also been one of the stock in trade items peddled on street corners by her former neighbour Martha Turner and her 'husband'. It had been Martha's murder that had first launched Esther into the search for her killer that had led to her meeting Jack, then a beat constable stationed in Whitechapel, and their subsequent joint enquiries had culminated the infamous 'Jack the Ripper' being put out of circulation. Somehow the powerful pomade smell brought back memories, but she had no time for idle reflection as she stood in the doorway and prepared to do her sales pitch.

'Who are you and what can I do for you?' the man behind the desk enquired in a cultured voice with a hint of femininity about it. His wing collar seemed to be strangling his scrawny neck and the cravat that he was wearing, despite the fact that they were rapidly going out of fashion, was so floral in pattern that he seemed to be talking to her from over the rim of a vase.

'My name's Esther Jacobs and I'm looking for work.'

'I take it that the exquisitely small hands that are no doubt snuggled inside those delightful calfskin gloves have never handled a hammer or saw?'

'No. I'm not a woodworker.'

'Then why are you seeking work through a union whose days are dedicated to securing employment for those who are?'

'I was working for a union until last week, but unfortunately my employer died.'

'Cancer? Bronchitis? Pneumonia?'

'She was murdered.'

'Helen Trenchard?'

'Yes,' Esther replied, somewhat taken aback. 'I had no idea that the news had travelled this far already.'

'Luton's hardly the ends of the earth, young lady,' Manners replied. 'Anyway, please take a seat on the chair you can see in front of you.'

In the centre of the extensive room was a large table whose primary function was probably as a resting place for tea things and there were four comfortable looking seats distributed around it. Esther took the nearest and George Manners got up from behind his desk and walked over to take the seat opposite hers.

'So what was your precise function with Miss Trenchard?'

'I was a general clerk,' Esther explained. 'I handled the filing of correspondence, the maintenance of membership records and the compiling of the accounts.'

'How many members?'

'Just under a thousand,' Esther lied, hoping that Manners would betray some knowledge of the fact that the membership levels had recently taken a fall due to the activities of Wally Mathewson, who may have been employed by the man who was now undressing her with his eyes.

'We have almost three times that number,' Manners advised her. 'It just so happens, as you may have noticed, that there's no-one on the front counter in the morning, due to the fact that the lady who occupies it in the afternoons — my fiancée, incidentally — has another morning job. This is a mere temporary arrangement, until such time as the union can afford her services fulltime and she no longer requires to supplement her income from other sources. Now tell me, what would be logically inappropriate were I to employ you in the mornings?'

Esther smiled sweetly as she replied. 'If you can't afford to employ *her* in the mornings, how could you afford to pay me?'

Manners smiled in what he no doubt regarded as a seductive way.

'Clever as well as beautiful. So my next obvious question is how little I would need to pay you.'

'I'm more interested in being employed than I am in being wealthy,' Esther replied, smiling back, reasonably confident that she had Manners' full attention. 'A pound a week would be sufficient at present, since it would more than cover my modest living expenses and my bus fares up and down Commercial Street.'

'Where do you live?'

'In the former Alliance offices in Lamb Street.'

'That converted tailors' workshop?'

'That's the one.' Esther smiled again, concealing her suspicions regarding the extent of the man's knowledge of the former Alliance. 'But only until June, then I shall be married and living in Clerkenwell.'

'May I take it that your intended is a man of considerable wealth who can afford the luxury of such a beautiful bride?'

'I'm not for sale,' Esther assured him, stung by the inference, but hoping that she hadn't gone too far. Fortunately Manners was still smiling.

'So what does this lucky man do?'

'He's a painter and decorator,' Esther lied, trying not to giggle at the mere thought.

'Well.' Manners leered as he looked down suggestively at the petticoats that were peeping out from under Esther's best grey costume. 'Your outstanding beauty might well be another handicap to your employment here. Those who call in here on business are working men, likely to be distracted by such a display of pulchritude on the front counter. More to the point, they might well begin to clog up the outer office area in order to admire it.'

'I've never found my looks to be a disadvantage,' Esther insisted, 'but I was rather hoping that a discerning employer would be more interested in my abilities.'

'Touché,' Manners replied in an almost girlish fashion as he clapped his hands lightly. 'You have spirit as well as beauty and might well be able to hold your own with men who would prefer you to hold theirs.'

Esther's blush was genuine and she only just suppressed the strong urge to lean across the table and smack the disgusting fop across the face. Instead she feigned a giggle of appreciation and Manners was sold.

'I'm prepared to give you a trial this morning,' he said, smiling, 'for which you will of course be paid. All I require of you is to enquire of any who come to your counter regarding the nature of their business, then come in here and advise me. The sight of you sashaying in here every few minutes will be well worth the experiment, but so far as concerns any more sustained employment, I'll need to speak to my fiancée, who is also a foundation officer of this union we have established between us. It is she who commands the front counter in the afternoons, as I already mentioned, and should you be employed more permanently, she will introduce you to the unfathomable mysteries of her records and her mastery of the telephone that you may have noticed on the front counter. For the present, if it rings, just pick it up with your delicate digits and say "Yes?". In my experience, the rest will follow naturally.'

Ten minutes later, Esther was installed on a high stool behind the front counter and soon grew accustomed to the brazen leers of the men who came in from time to time on business with George Manners. As she sat there, trying not to feel like the statue of Queen Victoria that sat proudly outside the hospital in Lambeth, she was able to organise her thoughts following her first conversation with her temporary employer.

First of all, he was everything that Helen Trenchard had described — an effeminate, arrogant, wet cheesecloth of a man who clearly regarded himself as a great catch for any lady. His languid and confident use of the English language betrayed a superior education somewhere well outside the narrow confines of Wapping and its largely illiterate residents, which in turn raised an important question regarding his interest in the growing trade union movement, unless he was one of those armchair Socialists who had begun to emerge, masking their naked political ambition behind a pretended concern for the working man. Helen had warned Esther against such people and Esther could now well understand why.

But of far greater significance was his apparent intimate knowledge of the Alliance and the premises it had occupied. So far as Esther could remember, the man had never been near the Lamb Street building and from what Helen had told her, her former employer's only connection with George Manners had been to hold him at arm's length and gently rebuff his amorous advances.

Of considerable concern to Esther right at this moment was the man's obvious knowledge of the fact that Helen had been murdered and *where*. It was unlikely that any London newspaper would have carried any account of a murder in distant Luton, an insignificant little place many miles to its north, so far as Esther knew, since she'd never been there. And even if the account of the murder had appeared in a small paragraph on an inside page, it was unlikely to have revealed the name of the victim.

On the other hand, Esther reasoned, one union might well take a keen interest in the affairs of another, not that the Alliance had been in any sense a rival to the one that George Manners and his fiancée had established. Esther smiled to herself as she tried to envisage the sort of woman who might find the man sufficiently attractive to want to marry him. Three hours later she no longer needed to employ her imagination.

She'd been idly reading one of the brochures that lay on the front counter, extolling the many benefits and advantages of being a member of the Woodworkers and Turners Union, when the street door flew open as if propelled by a siege catapult and a lady of formidable size and facial expression bore down on Esther as if she were a domestic caught in the act of stealing cutlery.

'Who the Hell are *you*?' the woman demanded.

'My name's Esther Jacobs,' Esther replied politely but firmly. 'Are you here to see Mr Manners?'

'You could say that,' the woman replied down her nose. 'I'm Margaret Templeton. On the assumption that you've already spoken with my fiancé and didn't just plomp your backside down behind the counter while resting between music hall engagements, did he get around to telling you that he was engaged to be married?'

'He did indeed,' Esther said, smiling back through gritted teeth, 'and I'm delighted to make your acquaintance.'

'My *brief* acquaintance,' Margaret insisted with seeming confidence. 'As George may also have got round to advising you, you're sitting where I normally sit.'

'In the afternoons, or so I was informed,' Esther replied sweetly, earning herself a snort of disagreement.

'Also in the mornings, with effect from the end of next month. You certainly won't be needed beyond that date, if indeed you're even required in the interim. You can go about your normal business once I've spoken with George. Any questions?'

'Yes.' Esther continued to smile. 'Is there a ladies' room?'

'Down to the left there.' Margaret nodded. 'Don't leave it in a mess.'

After making grateful use of the facilities, Esther tiptoed back out to the front entrance area, then slid back behind the front counter as she heard angry raised voices from Manners' office. She couldn't catch it all, but words such as 'trollop', 'hussy', 'shameless' and 'vacuous' were clearly audible and Esther was in no doubt that they were in reference to her, since they were coming from Margaret Templeton.

A few minutes later, a red faced Margaret flounced out of the inner office and glared at Esther.

'Three weeks and that's all. Is that understood?'

'Of course,' Esther replied, wondering within herself if she could tolerate three more weeks of this, before the penny dropped that she would only be there when Margaret wasn't.

'And keep your big dark eyes off my fiancé — is that also understood?'

'Perfectly,' Esther assured her meekly, suppressing the urge to burst out laughing at the mere suggestion.

'Right then, that's enough for today, so clear off. You'll only be getting ten shillings a week, so if you don't turn up tomorrow we'll quite understand.'

As the horse bus clomped its way northwards through the early afternoon traffic of Commercial Street, Esther looked briefly into Thrawl Street and up to the corner of George Street, where she'd once lived in a common lodging house, taking in sewing. Not even in those days would she have welcomed the attentions of anyone as crawlingly repulsive as George Manners, so Margaret Templeton had nothing to fear from her. As for George Manners, he might well come to regret being seduced by Esther's physical attraction into giving away something vital that could result in him finishing up dangling lifelessly on the end of a rope, like the piece of wet haddock that he resembled.

As she alighted from the bus and looked across Lamb Street towards her humble abode, she caught sight of Jack waiting by the front door. Excitedly she dodged through the traffic and threw her arms around him, planting a warm kiss on his lips and announcing with considerable pride, 'I got the job!'

To her considerable disappointment, his face fell.

'Ah. I came all the way down here to tell you that I've got tomorrow and Wednesday off in lieu of the days I lost last week. They've let me add this Thursday and Friday to them, so I've got four clear days to get on with the wallpapering and I was hoping that you'd be able to join me. Damn!'

Esther giggled at the sight of Jack so flustered and kissed him again.

'I'm only working in the mornings, so I can join you every day for dinner and then we can keep working all afternoon until the light fails. But from memory you've still got to strip off that first lot and burn it in the garden. That'll keep you going until dinner time tomorrow, then we can go and choose the new stuff.'

Jack looked hopefully into her eyes.

'Can we go and do that now? I can always pretend that I was inside here, looking for clues among the paperwork.'

'When we're married,' Esther said, smiling, 'I won't forget how glibly you can come up with excuses for being where you shouldn't. Have you had dinner yet?'

'No. I was hoping to take you to that Italian place just down the road there, although this time I'll stick to chicken.'

'So tell me what you've learned already,' Jack invited her as they sat side by side in the half empty trattoria, munching on chicken ciabatta. Esther pulled a face.

'George Manners has all the charm of a frog. No wonder Helen didn't welcome his overtures. But I suspect that he knows a great deal about Helen's death that he shouldn't. He knew that she'd been murdered and he knew where. Was it by any chance in the local papers here in London?'

'Not as far as I know,' Jack replied, 'but I'll obviously make enquiries. What exactly will you be doing down there?'

'Just sitting at the front counter, looking alluring and ignoring my new employer's nauseating attempts to get me interested in him.'

'You're *quite* sure you don't find him just the least bit attractive?' Jack asked with a worried frown.

'Not for as long as you're around. In fact, even if he were the last person on earth, I'd probably prefer to become a nun. In any case,' Esther added for good measure, 'the man's engaged to this dreadful dragon of a woman who clearly regards me as competition for her precious fiancé. If only she knew what I really think of him!'

'Will she give you a bad time all the same?'

Esther shook her head. 'No, as it happens we share the same job on the front counter. It seems that she has another job in the mornings, which is why George Manners requires me then, and she takes over at around dinner time when she gets back.'

It was late afternoon before they stood before their new front door, on the second floor landing of the residential building in Clerkenwell that would be their first matrimonial home, with or without wallpaper, in just over four months time. Jack was in the process of inserting the key in the lock, his feet surrounded by rolls of wallpaper and packets of paste that were guaranteed to be arsenic free, when they heard a light footfall on the staircase that gave access to the top floor. They both looked in the same direction as a late middle-aged lady appeared on the bottom stair dressed in slippers, a floor length skirt and a heavy woollen garment that might have once been her husband's.

'Are you the new people?' she enquired with an open smile.

'We will be after our wedding. This is Jack and I'm Esther. After June we'll both be called "Enright".'

'I'm Alice Bridges,' the lady advised them, 'and I live upstairs, alone since my husband died. It'll be *so* nice to have other people living here again. Do I gather from what's lying at your feet that you're here to do some decorating?'

'That's right,' Jack said as he pushed the door open and moved their purchases into their front hall.

'Do you have time for a cup of tea first?' Alice asked, and in the circumstances they felt that they couldn't refuse. A few minutes later they were sipping tea in Alice's kitchen and absorbing her life story.

'My husband Albert was a supervisor with the Board of Works,' she informed them, 'and he died coming up to two years ago. Pneumonia, it was, but he always had a weak chest. Then old Mrs Galway, the lady who used to live in the rooms you're taking over, fell ill with something unpronounceable, and I was privileged to be allowed to nurse her through her final days. She lived out her last few months in that front room of yours, so that she could watch the comings and goings in the street from her bed. It's been very quiet since she passed away, because the couple who have the ground floor are theatrical types and they're mostly away touring the country. Will you be using the rear garden much?'

'I will be tomorrow,' Jack said, grinning, 'since I have to burn off some old wallpaper. We only called in to drop off the new stuff, which we'll start hanging tomorrow.'

'I was hoping someone might take over the garden again,' Alice said wistfully. 'It was always so beautifully kept when my husband was alive and you get such a good view of it from the kitchen here. But just lately it's been allowed to fall into disuse and I'm not as good on my pins as I used to be, so perhaps Jack here could take up an interest in it.'

'I'll obviously do what I can,' Jack assured her, 'but I only get a limited amount of time off.'

'What do you do?'

'I'm a detective with Scotland Yard,' Jack replied proudly.

Alice smiled. 'That's reassuring to know. You aren't safe even in your own house these days and I'll feel better knowing that you're just downstairs.'

'And I work as a clerk for a trade union,' Esther added, not wishing to be written off yet.

'Very nice, dear, but that'll likely change when the babies come along.'

A few minutes later, back inside their own rooms, Jack felt free to express an opinion. 'A bit of a busybody, I reckon.'

'She's just lonely, Jack. And if the time comes when I'm stuck at home here, I may value the company.'

'I hope she doesn't expect too much of me in the garden.'

'Probably not as much as I expect of you in the way of wallpapering. You can make an early start in the morning and I'll be here with your dinner to see how much of the old stuff you've managed to remove. Then we can start with this new pattern. But now I really think you should at least pretend to be a detective on duty, while I get back to writing those boring letters to people who no doubt believe that the Alliance is still in existence. What's Uncle Percy doing in the meantime?'

'Checking on criminal histories. Mainly George Manners and people associated with him. What was the name of that woman he's engaged to?'

'Margaret Templeton, as far as I can remember. We didn't exactly become bosom friends in the few minutes that we had together before she all but threw me out of the office. I hope she keeps it that brief every day when we change shifts.'

The next three mornings in Wapping proved more or less uneventful for Esther, apart from two rather uncomfortable developments. On the Tuesday morning she arrived to find a beautiful vase of flowers on the front counter with a note written in a florid scrolling script that was the work of George Manners. He had signed his name above the message: 'They can't compare with your beauty, but they might cheer you up'. They lasted until dinner time, when Margaret Templeton arrived, took one look at the note and carried the vase into George's office, from which could be heard the voice of a very angry woman and the smashing of china. Esther opted to depart for the day without waiting for Margaret to re-emerge.

On the Wednesday, a bell appeared on the counter and once George presumably heard the sounds of Esther moving around behind it, he opened his office door and peered out.

'The bell is to alert you to the fact that you have an enquirer, should you be elsewhere.'

'You mean the ladies' room?'

George shook his head with a smile of pure butter. 'That, or inside with me, drinking tea. You *can* make tea, can't you?'

'Of course.'

'Then bring some in for us both at around ten thirty or so. The kitchen's down the hallway to the left and you'll find biscuits in the breadbin.'

Shortly after ten thirty, Esther found herself sitting across from George, pouring tea for them both. He was staring intently at her every action and Esther was on the point of inviting him to look elsewhere when he sighed.

'Such beauty and such delicate hand actions. You really are wasted sitting on a front desk. I've known women with only half your good looks rise very rapidly in commercial organisations such as ours. Are you not interested in something more suited to your natural attributes?'

'I'm happy as I am,' Esther replied evasively, in no doubt as to how George would like the conversation to develop.

'And of course, before much longer, you'll be lost to us in marriage. I hope your young man appreciates what he's getting. It's just a pity that he's not more established in society, so that he can supply you with all the material possessions that a young woman of your undoubted beauty deserves.'

'He's got everything I need,' Esther replied stiffly.

'For the moment, perhaps,' George argued. 'But once the babies come along and the first bloom of your youthful beauty fades, how can you be sure that his attentions won't wander? Some working men can be very fickle, you know. Far better that you hold yourself in readiness for someone who appreciates inner beauty — someone in a position to promote your own progress through society. I take it that the Alliance is now moribund?'

'Yes. I'm in the process of writing to all members and potential members to advise them of that sad fact.'

'Had you thought of promoting a union of your own? I could make that happen for you.'

'I'm sure you could, Mr Manners, but my only immediate ambition is marriage.'

'Call me George, please. And permit me to expand on how I believe we could move forward together in a whole new enterprise.'

Just then the front desk bell rang and Esther only just managed to suppress a yell of delight as she was able to use the excuse to rise from her chair and leave the office with a muted apology.

She was kept busy for the next hour or so with a seemingly endless line of men who all claimed that they needed to speak to George Manners urgently, but who gave the lie to that by appearing to be happy enough to lean on the counter while they waited and ogled Esther's every move. She was highly relieved when Margaret showed up and several of those with allegedly urgent business made their excuses and left.

However, the constant action at the counter had prevented Esther removing the tea things from the office and immediately after scowling at the bell on the counter, Margaret glared at Esther.

'I bet if I go in there I'll find evidence that you and George were taking tea together. And did he promise you the moon in a piecrust if you'd lie down for him? That's how he always begins — believe me, I've seen how he works. Just remember, my girl, that he's already engaged to me.' She looked swiftly round to ensure that they were alone, then whispered hoarsely. 'It's dinner time. *Bugger off.*'

At least Esther had the afternoons to look forward to and she cheered up and forgot the unpleasant mornings as she joined Jack in the excitement of their new home and together they explored the intricacies of wallpapering. Jack had almost completely stripped the wall of their first attempts, using a variety of tools he'd purchased from a sales assistant at a hardware shop who not only had the right equipment for such a task, but also gave Jack minute instructions regarding how wallpapering should be done.

'Is it all off?' Esther asked as she handed Jack the meat pie and bottle of ginger beer in the kitchen and nodded towards the closed bedroom door.

'All but one tiny piece under the window. I might need explosive for that. Once we've eaten, you can help me take it all downstairs and burn it.'

Just over an hour later, as they stood watching the smouldering pile in what had once been a rose bed, Jack gave Esther a wry smile.

'Don't look now, but Mrs Busybody from upstairs is watching our every move.'

'She's probably got nothing better to do with her time, Jack, so don't be too hard on her. It must be awful to be a lonely old widow.'

'I have a sneaking suspicion that she won't be lonely for long, once we move in and she has you available downstairs all day.'

'I'll probably be working during the day,' she reminded him.

'Perhaps, but hopefully not at that union place down in Wapping. Have you discovered anything worthwhile yet?'

'Only that George Manners fancies himself as a seducer of ladies, but I knew that already from what Helen was able to tell me about him. I'm a little surprised that he got himself engaged to that dreadful Margaret Templeton who helped him establish the union, since according to Helen he still held a burning torch for her. But having met the woman, I can well imagine how a mild-mannered little pansy like him could be terrorised into an engagement. She's really horrible and has taken a strong dislike to me since George began paying me serious attention.'

'But you've neither seen nor heard anything to connect Manners with either the intimidating actions of Wally Mathewson or Helen's murder?'

'Absolutely nothing. But talking of lack of progress, can we just leave this to smoulder out and go back upstairs and start on the new stuff?'

'Yes, why not? I've picked up a few handy hints on how to do it. Prepare to be amazed by your fiancé's skill as a paper hanger.'

While Jack was demonstrating his new skills to Esther they heard a heavy knock on their front door.

'If that's the nosy cow from upstairs, tell her we died.'

'Really, Jack!' Esther admonished him. 'You're going to have to learn to be more neighbourly to poor old Alice.'

'"Poor old Alice", as you call her, has a strong enough knock. Go and chase her away.'

Esther scurried down the hall, opened the door, then looked up, wide-eyed.

'Uncle Percy! What a welcome surprise! Do come in.'

Percy followed her down the hallway and into the designated bedroom in which Jack was pasting his first sheet, face down on the old kitchen table that had been abandoned by Mrs Galway's heirs and successors after her death.

'Glad we found some use for your talents,' Percy grinned. 'Your next job is to fix a lock on that street door. Anyone could walk in and then they only have to get past the door to your rooms.'

'Shouldn't you be on duty?' Jack growled.

'I *am* on duty,' Percy replied as his face suddenly adopted a serious expression. 'How soon before this place is fit for Esther to move in?'

'Forever, if we keep getting these interruptions,' Jack replied with irritation. 'What's the hurry, all of a sudden?'

'I've just completed the next stage in our investigations, down in Lambeth,' Percy replied with a frown. 'What I've learned is very disturbing and the sooner Esther's out of Lamb Street the happier I'll be.'

Chapter 24

Percy Enright had been very busy during the past few days, making a pain of himself in various cobwebbed corners of the police service. He was determined to track down Helen Trenchard's killer, but had little to go on other than the name of the woman who had found her body — 'Marjory Collins' — and a vague description of her being in her mid thirties. That was somewhere to start, although he never felt entirely comfortable working south of the river, which for all police officers seemed like a psychological brick wall. Either you were a 'north of the river' copper, or you preferred the south side and for a 'northerner' like Percy, the south side was something of a closed book.

On the Tuesday morning after their return from Luton — well over a week since Helen's murder — he'd stood staring thoughtfully into the tanner's yard in Merrow Street. The lady who'd given the obviously false name of Marjory Collins might well have known this area, and this address, well. Well enough to fool the police in Luton, anyway. Had she just got lucky when she correctly picked the name of a Lambeth street, or had she known that although the street existed, they would only find a tanner's yard when they checked on the address of number 27?

As he stared into the yard, his attention was drawn to a building at the back of it that looked as if it was lived in, or might perhaps once have been. It was normal for tradesmen such as tanners, who plied their trade in a yard of some sort, to live adjacent to them, often in a house that went with the business. It was a long shot, but someone living here might know of a Marjory Collins. He crossed the street and walked into the yard, wrinkling his nose against the rank smell of whatever they used to cure the cow-hide, which he vaguely remembered might be excrement. It certainly smelt like it and he was anxious to minimise his enquiries in this particular locality.

A tired looking man gazed up at him with rheumy eyes from the barrel in which he was stirring God knew what with the aid of a long wooden paddle.

'Can I 'elp yer, friend?' the man enquired.

'I hope so,' Percy replied, holding his police badge high in the air, wondering if the smell by which he was surrounded might somehow tarnish it. 'I'm looking for a Marjory Collins. Could be a "Mrs" or a "Miss", but "Marjory Collins" anyway.'

'Never 'eard of anybody o' that name,' the man replied.

Percy nodded towards what he took to be the house at the rear of the yard. 'Who lives there?'

'Me an' the missus. The children moved out years ago; not interested in takin' over the business their old man worked 'is arse off ter leave 'em. Why d'yer wanna know?'

'How long have you lived there?'

'Most o' me life. Me old man took over the business when the bloke what owned it died. Murdered, they reckon. By 'is own children, what's more.'

'What was the name of the man who was murdered — the former owner of the business?'

'No idea, my friend. I were only a young bloke at the time. Goin' on twenty, I musta bin. Then me old man died o' that cholera what come through 'ere in the seventies an' I only just escaped it meself. I'm comin' on fifty now, so yer talkin' maybe thirty odd years ago when we moved in 'ere. Say eighteen sixty or thereabouts — does that 'elp yer?'

'Perhaps and perhaps not. Thank you anyway. Where's the local police station?'

'I thought yer said yer was a copper? No wonder they don't come when yer need 'em, if they don't even know where their own bleedin' station is. If yer go back down this street, then take the bus up Walworth Road 'til yer on Kennington Lane, then it's a few yards down on yer left.'

It was Percy's first foray into Lambeth Police Office, the central focal point of 'L Division' of the Metropolitan Police, and after flashing his Yard badge and making it sound urgent, he was eventually sitting in front of Inspector Makepeace.

'I would have been a young constable in those days,' Makepeace smiled benignly, 'but I can sort of remember it, because it was so unusual. The man who died was a right old bastard, even for this area in those days. Beat his wife and children for daily exercise, drank like it was his religion, got himself locked up in here for "D and D" every Friday night, you know the sort. Or are they all law-abiding churchgoers on your patch?'

'My patch is notionally the whole of the Met,' Percy reminded him with a smile, 'so you don't have to draw me a diagram. I'm told by the man who owns the business now that the previous occupant was murdered by his own children. That correct?'

'So they reckon, but it was never proved and quite frankly nobody cared. We all but had a party the night it happened and we looked the other way. Mind you, we needed to, 'cos he was a right mess to look at. Forty odd knife wounds, they reckoned, but of course, with it being a tanner's business, there was no shortage of leather knives lying around.'

'And the children?'

'A boy and a girl. They may have been twins, because I remember that they were roughly the same age. They were taken in by neighbours, but they repaid the community pretty poorly.'

'In what way?'

'Well, for a start, the boy turned into a really nasty piece of work, if you were a young girl, that is. He was done a few times for burglary and indecent assault and narrowly escaped an attempted rape. Then he disappeared into the woodwork — ten years or so ago, it must have been.'

'This is a real shot in the dark, but his name wasn't by any chance Wally Mathewson, was it?'

The inspector's face lit up in recognition.

'That was it — Mathewson! The father's name was Albert, I remember him well enough now. A real criminal family, if ever there was one, and *she* certainly kept up the family tradition.'

'The daughter?'

'Yes, her. She got married pretty young and after a while her husband got tired of her, because she wasn't exactly an oil painting. Then she caught him playing an away game with the woman a few doors down and all Hell broke loose. She got off the murder charge because she persuaded the jury — who must have felt sorry for her — that she'd strangled her old man in self defence when he went for her in this almighty fight that woke up two blocks of neighbours. I didn't believe it and neither did anyone else in this station, but there's no accounting for juries, is there?'

'Do you remember her name?'

'We charged her under her married name — the same name as her victim. Can't remember it now, but it was only a few years back, so we should find her in records.'

'Without a surname to go on?'

'We file them by crime, as well. At least, we cross-reference them, so all we have to do is go back through the "Murder" file and that'll give us her name. Then we can pull the file from the alphabetical pile.'

'We?'

'Yes, why not? I know the old cases better than most, given that I've been in this station all my police career, and as soon as we hit the name it'll all come back to me. If you come back in an hour, I might have something more for you.'

'Can I bring you back a meat pie or something?' Percy asked gratefully and Makepeace smiled and tapped his stomach.

'Ulcer, I'm afraid. It's boiled eggs and cheese sandwiches only for me, according to the doctor, but thanks anyway.'

Outside, Percy was too nervous to eat, so he walked up and down the busy thoroughfare smoking one pipe after another. He heard a distant clock chime two and went back into the police station, where the desk sergeant waved him over to his barred window.

'Yer the bloke from the Yard what were in 'ere earlier, ain't yer? The Inspector said ter show yer this file when yer come back in. I'll need ter ask yer fer some identification first, I'm afraid.'

Percy handed across his police badge, accepted the file and took it to the empty public bench across from the charge desk. Slightly trembling, he read the front cover and learned that the woman who had narrowly escaped the gallows for the strangling murder of her cheating husband was called Marjory Collins. That had been in 1892 and by then most police stations had adopted the practice of photographing their suspect when they were first arrested. If this file contained a photograph, he could sign for it and take it up to Luton and ask them if this was the woman using that same name who'd reported the finding of Helen Trenchard's body.

With fumbling fingers he flipped through the pages to the first entry — the one at the back of the file that contained the photograph. The desk sergeant looked up out of curiosity as he heard Percy give a yell of triumph.

He didn't need to travel to Luton to pinch this particular lady. Just a mile or so back north across the river.

Chapter 25

'Why wouldn't Uncle Percy tell us why it was so important that I move out of Lamb Street?' Esther asked on the Wednesday as she and Jack proudly surveyed the first fully papered wall in the fading light. 'At any event, it'll have to wait until we get a bed installed.'

'A double bed,' Jack reminded her.

She smiled. 'Don't think for one moment that you can visit me at night once I move in here. If anything, it only encourages me to stay where I am. You don't have a spare key to Lamb Street.'

'All the same, the sooner the better, to judge by the look on Uncle Percy's face. He's obviously found out something important and didn't even want to tell me, presumably because he needs to confirm it in some way and didn't want to unduly alarm you. I won't be seeing him for the next two days, because I'll be busy finishing off this room, but I think we should take heed of what he was warning us.'

'Then the sooner we get on with this, the better,' Esther replied. 'I'm glad we had to change it for the good of our health — those rose clusters are really pretty and not so difficult to line up on the edges.'

'We should have this room finished by the time we knock off on Friday,' Jack predicted. 'After we give it the weekend to dry off, we can go looking for the bed and the sheets that go on it. Then you can move in.'

'If you insist,' Esther agreed. 'But that'll mean that I'll have to take the bus down to Wapping every day.'

'Except Thursdays and Fridays, if you can wangle it,' Jack reminded her. 'Those will be my days off until the shift rosters are changed again, then it'll be back to Sunday dinners at Barking, but without Uncle Percy.'

'Don't remind me,' Esther replied with a grimace. 'Can't we just plead that we're busy decorating?'

'If we try that, Mother will insist on coming down here to supervise in order to speed things up and everything will finish up in her favourite blue. How long do you think you'll need to finish off that work for the Alliance, anyway?'

'Another couple of weeks, I'd guess. Then I'll be free every afternoon to come back here and wallpaper.'

On the Friday morning, Esther came to an abrupt halt in the doorway of the union office and stared at the front counter. Behind it sat Margaret Templeton, with a facial expression that resembled a tree-feller's double handed saw. She looked up briefly as she saw Esther rooted to the spot, then looked back down at the counter and sneered.

'Ten shillings, wasn't it? I'm just counting it out for you, then you can go back out where you came from.'

'I beg your pardon?' Esther demanded.

'You don't work here any more,' Margaret told her with an unpleasant smile that was directed towards the counter. 'I handed in my notice at my other place of employment yesterday, so we don't need you today — or ever again.'

'That's not necessarily the case,' George advised them both as he emerged from his office, having heard the sound of the two women talking. 'I have in mind promoting the union outside London and I thought that Esther and I might put together some sort of presentation that we can make to groups of potential members in cities up and down the country.'

'You'll be doing no such thing!' Margaret shouted. 'Don't think I haven't been aware of your tongue drooling like a cat with a fish head every time this little baggage shows her face in here! You don't want to travel up and down the country with her — you just want to travel up and down her garters, you dirty old goat!'

'You can't speak to Miss Jacobs like that, as if she's some sort of cheap tart!' Manners protested.

Margaret's face rapidly turned crimson as she yelled back at him. 'Can I not? Well just remember this, George Manners. You and I are up to our necks in all this and if you think for one moment that you can abandon me for the first bit of fluff that sticks her bosom in your face, then you can think again! You're going to marry me like you promised and if you step one foot over the line you'll regret it when you find your feet inside Newgate instead. Now tell this tottie where she gets off — or do you want me to throw her out on her arse?'

'Don't either of you trouble yourselves on my account,' Esther replied haughtily. 'I'm just leaving. I hope never to see either of you again.'

With that she turned and walked sedately out of the door, quickening her pace as she headed for the bus stop.

Once safely on the bus, Esther took it all the way to its terminus at Liverpool Street Station, then changed to a direct service down to Charing Cross, from where she knew she could walk along the Embankment to Scotland Yard. It was almost dinner time before she sat down, exhausted, on a bench in front of the slowly churning river, having been informed that Detective Sergeant Enright was out on enquiries and that no-one knew when he was likely to be back. She rested for a few minutes, then walked back to Charing Cross and took the

Farringdon service bus that she knew ran through Clerkenwell on its loop through the inner northern suburbs.

It was mid afternoon before she handed the late dinner to Jack with an apology, then all but staggered through to the kitchen and flopped down in the only chair.

'Sorry I'm so late, but I've got something important to report.'

'So have I,' Jack grinned. 'The bedroom wallpaper's finished. Come and take a look.'

'In a minute, Jack. I'm exhausted after travelling all the way to Scotland Yard, only to find that Uncle Percy isn't there and they don't know when he'll be back.'

'So what did you find out?'

'George Manners and Margaret Templeton all but admitted that they were behind all those burglaries. They got into a big argument over me — and I'm dismissed from there, by the way — and then Margaret let fly something about Manners finishing up in Newgate and that whatever it was, they were in it together.'

'Do you think that included Helen's murder?'

'No idea, but we have to tell Percy without delay.'

'I'll do that tomorrow and we'll probably both come down to Lamb Street to get more details from you. Now come and see where you'll be sleeping when the wallpaper dries out.'

'Quite frankly, the way I feel at the moment, I could sleep on the floor in there. But never let it be said that I didn't give you support and encouragement.'

Her eyes opened wide as she took in the finished room and the tiredness seemed to be consigned to memory.

'Oh Jack, it's beautiful!' she breathed. 'I can't wait to move in!'

'Next week, I reckon,' Jack replied proudly. 'And now that you have no other distractions, you can finish down at the Alliance and move up here. That'll please me as well as Uncle Percy, wherever he is.'

While his whereabouts were being guessed at, Percy was back at Scotland Yard, cursing loudly. His grand entrance into the premises of Hemmingsworth Properties in the company of two uniformed constables had netted one suspect, but not the important one.

Two hours earlier he'd strode purposefully into the front office and demanded to speak to Timothy Bowden. When the man had emerged, Percy had informed him that he was under arrest.

'What for?' Bowden demanded. 'Haven't we met before?'

'We have indeed, Mr Bowden, and on that occasion we discussed how a team of joiners headed by a bogus foreman supplied by you had conducted certain internal alterations inside premises in Lamb Street, Spitalfields, of which your company is the landlord. By this means you obtained an unauthorised list of members of the Alliance that was occupying those premises, thereby facilitating a series of burglaries carried out by a man called Walter Mathewson. A man whose sister you also employ here, no doubt under the assumed name of "Marjory Collins". Where is she, by the way?'

'She's no longer employed here,' Bowden advised him. 'She resigned with effect from yesterday.'

'Do you have her home address?'

'I assume so, although I'd need to consult our records.'

'Do it. Now,' Percy instructed him.

Bowden opened a filing cabinet to the side of the inner office in which a young female employee sat, open-mouthed at the dramatic turn of events on an otherwise dull Friday afternoon.

'Here we are.' Bowden smiled hopefully as he handed Percy the employment application letter.

Percy took one look at it, then snorted in disgust.

'I spent an interesting morning at that Lambeth address, Mr Bowden,' he snarled. 'As if you didn't already know, it's a tanners' yard and Marjory Collins — or Marjory Mathewson, as she was born — hasn't lived there since she was a child, and she and her brother — the man you were persuaded to employ as a bogus joinery foreman — knifed their father to death some thirty odd years ago. The same lady also committed a callous murder in Luton two weeks ago that has deprived you of a long-term tenant for your Lamb Street premises.'

'I know nothing of any murders!' Bowden protested.

Percy nodded. 'I'm prepared to believe that, for the time being anyway. But you're under arrest for being an accessory to burglary. Take him out, constables.' He looked back at the white face of the girl in the office. 'Don't let it upset you, my dear. Fridays can be a pain sometimes. If it's any consolation, I used up two of my days off preparing for this.'

Esther unlocked the front door to the Alliance building with a light heart, knowing that she wouldn't be living there for much longer. She was a good way through the pile of correspondence that she had set herself to conduct, she had obtained all the information she could regarding George Manners and his union, and on Jack's next days off they would be choosing the bed in which she'd begin married life with him.

She went into the kitchen, made herself a cup of tea, then decided on a whim to venture downstairs with the lamp and collect some more correspondence, which she took back to the kitchen and began writing. The sooner she started on the last of the letters, the sooner she could get on with choosing furniture and working fulltime on preparing the rooms in Clerkenwell in which her future awaited her.

After an hour or so she felt her head nodding with the exhaustion of all the day's excitement and she decided to call it a night. She took the lamp and walked the few steps down the hallway into her bedroom, climbed into her night dress, smiled lovingly at the wedding dress hanging from a hook on the wall, and fell almost instantly asleep.

Percy finally tracked Jack down at his lodgings in Farringdon, having wasted a valuable hour looking for him in both Clerkenwell and Spitalfields.

'Where's Esther?' Percy demanded.

Jack looked back at him fearfully. 'Isn't she in Lamb Street? That's where she said she was going; she was exhausted after running around looking for you at the Yard and she claims to have the evidence we need against Manners and his union crowd.'

'That may explain it,' Percy replied, obviously agitated. 'I hammered on the door until it threatened to come off its hinges, but there was no response. Hopefully she's safely tucked up in bed.'

'What's all the urgency, anyway?' Jack enquired, now thoroughly alarmed.

'I've identified Helen Trenchard's killer, but she's still on the loose,' Percy explained. 'She was working at Hemmingsworth Properties, which explains the link between them and the attacks on union members. The name she's using now is

"Marjory Collins", but before that she was "Marjory Mathewson". Name ring a bell?'

'Damn,' was Jack's only response.

'It's worse than that,' Percy explained breathlessly. 'As Marjory Mathewson, she and her brother Wally knifed their parents to death. Then, as Marjory Collins she strangled her husband of that name when he proved unfaithful to her.'

'Wasn't Marjory Collins the name of the woman who allegedly found Helen's body in Luton?'

'She obviously didn't just "find" it — she created it,' Percy replied, grim faced. 'She also has a spare key to Lamb Street.'

'We had the locks changed, didn't we?'

'Yes, but a copy of the key was supposed to be delivered to Hemmingsworth Properties, in accordance with the terms of the lease. We have to assume that this was done.'

'So what now? Head down to Lamb Street and break the door down? It'll give Esther the fright of her life if we pull a trick like that.'

'She won't have a life left if Marjory Collins gets to her first. I've got a police wagon and a couple of constables outside. I'm off back down to Lamb Street and I thought you'd want to come with me.'

Less than thirty minutes later the police wagon was drawn up immediately outside the door of the former Alliance office and two uniformed constables were standing on the narrow pavement outside the front door. Percy pushed his head through the open carriage window and looked carefully up and down the street.

'No sign of Marjory Collins. Hopefully when she sees the police wagon she'll stay away. Looks like we got here in time.'

He was almost fatally wrong.

Chapter 26

Esther was experiencing a recurring nightmare from five years previously, when her adoptive home with the Rosens in their Lamb Street bespoke tailoring emporium had been the target of a vicious anti-Semitic attack and almost reduced to a shell by the fire that had engulfed it. In her troubled sleep, she twisted and turned, her head moving from one side of the pillow to another as she sought to avoid the smoke, then ran, clad only in her nightdress, down the staircase from the second floor, just before the staircase crashed behind her in a shower of glittering embers and she was pulled out into the street by Isaac, who had been waiting near the front door, after bellowing to her that she had to get out immediately or lose her life.

She came awake to a violent coughing fit and quickly became aware that the smoke was real, rather than a nightmare. She tried to get downstairs, but the staircase was already consumed by flames. In a flash of memory Esther recalled the old service hoist that she had played on as a child, when she accompanied her parents to the Rosen building to deliver the cloth that they imported. It was basically a rope pulley that could be operated from either the upper or lower floor, or — as a very young Esther had demonstrated more than once, to her parents' consternation — by a person sitting on the platform and pulling on the rope to its side.

She slid out of bed and hurried to the doorway, then stopped in her tracks, turned back and grabbed the wedding dress from the hook.

Esther climbed onto the platform, which luckily had last been used some years ago to transport small items of furniture up to Isaac and Ruth's old bedroom — the one from which Esther was now fleeing for her life. Holding the wedding dress tightly to her, she reached out with one hand and began pulling upward on the rope as the platform creaked and groaned into life following several years of disuse. Slowly it cranked down foot by foot, until the ground floor came into sight and Esther leaped down from the platform, holding her wedding dress before her like a battle banner.

While Esther had been making her escape, Jack and Percy had been both busy and successful. They had been sitting in the coach, watching the front door intently, when it had opened to reveal the scurrying figure of Marjory Collins as she alighted onto the pavement outside, into the arms of two uniformed police constables. It was arguable which of them was the most surprised.

'Hold on to that woman!' Percy yelled as he jumped from the coach and, from his jacket pocket, extracted the restraints that he placed on her wrists before forcing her to the ground. Jack jumped out after him and stared, horror-stricken, at the sight through the still open door.

'Get the Fire Brigade!' he yelled to the constables who had stood back to allow Percy room to move and one of them raced off down the road. A few minutes later they heard the familiar clanging of a bell as a horse drawn fire wagon raced up Commercial Street and almost skidded into Lamb Street. Three men in full fire fighting uniform jumped down from it and while two of them attached a hose of some sort to the huge water container, the third man raced inside armed with an axe and headed for the burning staircase.

He was stopped dead in his tracks as he became aware, to his right, of a pale white figure stumbling towards him through the smoke. He took it at first to be a ghost, until it occurred to him that ghosts don't cough and he realised that he was staring at a woman in her nightdress weaving her way through clouds of smoke, bearing a long white garment aloft, as if trying to preserve it from any smoke or flame.

From Esther's perspective, it looked as if a knight in shining armour had come to rescue her, until she realised that the battle helm that was glinting in the reflection from the flames that had engulfed the staircase was in fact the silver helmet of a fireman. She called out to him just as Jack staggered through the door with his face covered by his handkerchief as a protection against the swirling smoke, heard Esther's voice and swerved to his right to collect her in his arms. He guided her to the pavement and was about to lead her to the coach when she looked down towards the ground where Percy had a woman pinioned.

'That's Margaret Templeton!' she cried out.

'I'll get you next time!' Margaret yelled up at her, before Percy shook her into silence.

'One of several aliases,' he advised Esther with a grin. 'As "Marjory Collins" she murdered Helen — and a few other people, in her time.'

'Are you alright?' Jack demanded as he turned Esther towards him in order to look into her eyes.

'I think so,' Esther replied in a feeble voice. 'I saved my wedding dress — look.'

As she held the dress out towards him, the delayed shock took over and she crumpled to the ground.

Chapter 27

Esther woke the next morning to find herself in a comfortable warm bed, with Lucy smilingly placing tea things on a side table, Jack sitting on the side of her bed holding her hand and looking longingly into her eyes and Percy standing by the back wall looking smug.

'Thank God you're still with us,' Jack choked as he leaned forward and kissed her gently on the forehead.

'I wasn't thinking of going anywhere,' Esther joked back weakly. 'I vaguely remember calling for my wedding dress.'

'Hanging up there, in front of the window, to get the smell of smoke out of it,' Lucy reassured her with a nod, adding, 'It's absolutely beautiful and far too good to miss your happy day.'

Esther smiled with satisfaction as she turned her head to look up at the precious garment swinging gently in the slightly chill breeze from the open window.

'Thank you, Lucy. Is this your house?'

'It is. It's also your home until you're strong enough to move into your new accommodation in Clerkenwell. And before that you'll need to build up your strength to go round the stores with Jack, buying furniture.'

As the recent memories came flooding back, Esther looked across at Percy.

'You got Margaret Templeton, didn't you? Was that *last* night?'

'It was indeed.' Percy smiled down at her. 'Also known as Marjory Mathewson and Marjory Collins and it was she who murdered Helen. She'd obviously come after you and had poured paraffin all over the bottom stairs before throwing a match into it. You were lucky to escape.'

'Can either you or Percy explain why Margaret Templeton wanted to murder me as well as Helen? Surely, with the Alliance finished, she had no further issue with me?'

Percy coughed slightly with embarrassment before explaining.

'That was all my fault, I'm afraid, but you nearly died for the same reason as Helen. It had nothing to do with the Alliance, as it turns out. Marjory Collins, to give her the name under which she's been charged with murder and attempted murder, would seem to be a bit ... well, a bit "loony", if you'll pardon that uncaring description. She's no great beauty, as you will have concluded for yourself and she's sensitive to the point of mania about holding on to any man who shows her any interest. Some years ago now, when her husband was unfaithful to her, she strangled the life out of him, but managed to plead self-defence and play the sympathy card with a jury. Then a couple of years ago she fell in with George Manners, who couldn't resist plying her with charm in order to seduce her. Then he found that she wouldn't let go and when he became obsessed with Helen it was all too much for poor old Marjory.'

'Hardly "poor old Marjory",' Jack protested. 'She's a deranged killer and if we hadn't got to her when we did, Esther wouldn't be here today.'

'We?' Percy challenged him, and Esther felt obliged to step in with something diversionary.

'So the union thing was just a coincidence, was it?'

Percy shook his head.

'Not for George Manners, it wasn't. He was hoping to improve his standing in the wider union world by nipping the

Alliance in the bud and it was Marjory who introduced him to her very unpleasant brother Wally Mathewson, an adept burglar with a sick obsession with ladies' undergarments. The perfect man to deliver the typewritten warnings that Marjory produced while working in the Hemmingsworth office, which she instructed her revolting brother to deliver, with a disgusting sideline of his own for added emphasis in the case of those members who were important to the Alliance.'

'Have you arrested Manners yet?' Esther enquired.

Percy nodded with a smile.

'In the early hours of this morning. I'm planning to tip him upside down later, but I suspect that Helen was unwise enough to share far too much information with him regarding how the Alliance was expanding.'

'You should let Esther rest now,' Lucy suggested as she handed her the cup of tea she'd just poured. 'And aren't you two supposed to be on duty?'

'I'll be going down to Wapping to interview Mr Manners,' Percy advised them, 'then I think I've earned the rest of the day off. But I'll definitely be behind my desk at the Yard tomorrow, if only to avoid going to Barking.'

'And I'll think of some constabulary reason why I have to begin painting our new front room, before coming down here to keep you company while Lucy and Teddy go to worship at the shrine.' Jack smiled at Esther. 'White again?'

Esther nodded, then looked up at Lucy.

'Will you please give your mother my apologies for yet again missing her delicious Sunday dinner and explain to her why I need to rest for a day or two?'

Lucy chuckled. 'Why is everybody so scared of my mother? I'll certainly pass on your message, Esther, but once she hears that her precious daughter-in-law to be is indisposed, she'll be down here like a shot.'

'Oh no!' Esther groaned.

Lucy placed a comforting hand on her shoulder.

'You've no need to fear her biting tongue, Esther. It's all for show and she really thinks the world of you.'

That point was dramatically underlined late on the Sunday evening, when the bedroom door opened and Lucy's head appeared round it, looking slightly apprehensive.

'Just checking that you two weren't at it in my absence, because you have a visitor who wouldn't be amused.'

She stepped to one side and Constance Enright swept in.

'My *dearest* Esther,' she cooed as she leaned down to kiss her, 'when Lucy told me all about your dreadful experience, I simply *had* to come back with them in the coach and see for myself that you were still alive and blooming. What a terrible ordeal it must have been and while I'd expect nothing else from Percy, I'm amazed, and frankly very disappointed, to hear that Jackson went along with it. And why aren't you at work, Jackson? Wasn't that your excuse for not visiting me in Barking yet again?'

'I've just clocked off, Mother, and naturally I wanted to check on Esther, since she's been on her own all day, as everyone else in this house was obeying your summons.'

'That'll be enough cheek, Jackson. Off you go and leave the ladies to speak privately.'

Jack gave Esther a chaste kiss, then wandered out through the bedroom door, passing Lucy in the hallway with his arms spread and his face set in a 'could you not have prevented this?' look. Lucy shrugged him an apology in return, then went back into the bedroom to offer Esther some moral support. With a shock she discovered that Constance was admiring the wedding dress still hanging in the window, with no idea that Esther had made it herself.

'Such *exquisite* embroidery,' Constance was oozing. 'It must have cost an absolute fortune. Is it West End?'

'Actually,' Esther lied glibly, 'it's a very exclusive designer I know from my earlier days in the trade, and I'm sworn to secrecy in return for their agreeing to produce just this one garment.'

'What do you think, Lucy?' Constance enquired of her daughter, who was experiencing considerable difficulty in maintaining a straight face. 'Wouldn't it be simply *wonderful* if we could get matching dresses for Alice and Elizabeth?'

'Who are they?' Esther asked disingenuously, trying not to grin.

'Your new bridesmaids, dear, didn't Lucy tell you? She's in the family way, if you didn't know that either and clearly can't expect to be looking her best in June, so I thought that Alice and Elizabeth would be perfect substitutes. They're my sister Jane's two girls and *quite* the young ladies. They'd look absolutely *perfect* in matching dresses to yours, so could you weave your magic on your old friend?'

'I could try, of course,' Esther replied evasively, 'but ...'

'Good, then that's decided,' Constance interrupted. 'Just let me know when the girls will be needed in the West End to be measured. They live out in Buckinghamshire, you see, so we'll need to make special arrangements for them to travel.'

'Actually,' Esther offered, seizing the wonderful opportunity that had opened up, 'if you'd like to send them here, then assuming that the designer would be prepared to oblige, I could measure the girls myself. I'm quite accustomed to doing that sort of thing and it would give me an opportunity to get to know the girls you've chosen as my bridesmaids.'

'An excellent notion!' Constance declared, then turned to Lucy. 'We mustn't let Esther get too fatigued, dear, so we should perhaps go down to supper now. Will Edward be joining us?'

With a knowing wink over her mother's shoulder back at Esther, Lucy began to lead the way out of the bedroom, before Constance turned and smiled back at the invalid.

'I'll be sure to look in on you again before I leave, Esther dear, so don't be despondent. I'm only concerned that you don't make yourself ill again with all the excitement.'

Esther managed to suppress the flow of nervous giggles until the door had been firmly shut, but she was still grinning half an hour later when Lucy popped back in with a huge smile on her face.

'That was brilliantly done, Esther. Mother's spent the whole of supper telling Teddy how she's arranged for a secret designer, who probably takes commissions from the Queen in her spare time, to make matching dresses for Alice and Elizabeth.'

'When does she leave?' Esther asked anxiously.

'First thing tomorrow morning, because she has her regular Ladies' Guild meeting in the afternoon, so don't worry on that score.'

'Thank you for organising for Alice and Elizabeth to be my bridesmaids.'

'Think nothing of it, since it was the simplest thing in the world. I just mentioned that they might be a good choice and within thirty seconds it had become Mother's idea in the first place and was beyond all argument.'

Epilogue

Esther stared intently over the vicar's balding head towards the image of Christ Crucified that was hanging off the back wall, in an attempt to hold back the tears of happiness. As the wedding service droned on in her ear, she gave her own thanks to God for the changes in her life that at one time she would have regarded as mere fantasy. A loving man standing nervously by her side, and on his other side the best uncle-in-law that anyone could wish for. She could even ignore the occasional sniffle from the row behind, from the woman who was about to become her mother-in-law, supported on one arm by a radiant Lucy who was diplomatically feeding her handkerchiefs.

Esther listened attentively to the vows that Jack was taking, since it would be her turn next. Finally she got there, when the man in the rather badly repaired clerical robes pronounced them man and wife and they walked proudly arm in arm through the front door of the church and back out into a perfect June day, where some irritating little drip was playing around with a camera and periodically disappearing under a black cloth that was a distinct improvement in his appearance.

Two hours later, on the back lawn and into their fourth glass of champagne each, Jack and Percy were engaged in a pleasant exchange of unpleasantries as they went back through the precise terms of the best man's speech that had been mercifully short and mercilessly accurate. Constance Enright sauntered up to Esther like an ocean-going galleon with no rudder and breathed champagne all over her as she embraced her in a maternal hug that felt more like an assault.

'*Dearest* Esther,' she slurred. 'Welcome to the family at long last. You've made Jackson *so* happy, which is all that I ever required of any wife he chose, but you're *so* talented as well.'

'I am?' Esther queried.

Constance tapped her nose with her free hand.

'You made those dresses, didn't you? Lucy let it slip out. Your secret's safe with me, provided you agree to make my gown for the Harvest Festival Ball.'

'I'd be honoured,' Esther replied, then caught Jack's eye as he waved her over.

'Uncle Percy's organised our coach to the station, so better go and collect your bags for the honeymoon,' he advised her as he looked her up and down and she felt a hot flush run through her system.

They stepped into the coach amid shouts of encouragement, well wishes for the future and yet more confetti. As the coach began to trundle down the laneway, with the hatch still open to allow in a breeze to moderate the heat of the late afternoon sun, Jack shouted up to the coachman. 'I take it that you know the way to the station?'

'Course I do,' the coach driver replied. 'But I'm goin' a bit further than that, arn' I?'

'How do you mean?' Jack enquired.

'Well, someone back there — a tall bloke 'e were, an' smokin' a pipe — 'e slipped me a twenty ter take yer ter Southend. That's right, in't it?'

'Yes,' Jack chuckled, 'that's right.' He sat back down next to Esther and gave her a huge kiss. 'I can do that, now that you're "Mrs Enright". Just don't become as bossy as the other one.'

'If you don't behave yourself, Jackson Enright,' Esther purred in a perfect imitation of the lady in question, 'our coach driver will get more than twenty pounds as a reward for his trouble. Although he'd probably fall off his seat if he saw us both with no clothes on inside his coach.'

A NOTE TO THE READER

Dear Reader,

I hope that you enjoyed this second book in the series of Esther and Jack investigations. They demanded that I write it.

Most novelists will tell you that there comes an unnerving point at which their characters commandeer their lives. You are allowed time off to eat, drink, sleep and discharge a minimum of domestic duties, but otherwise you discover that you have created a burden on your conscience equivalent to a nagging spouse or a whining, needy child. If you have left them dangling off a tall building, or being held at gunpoint, they will keep prodding your waking – and sometimes sleeping – brain to hurry up and get them out of there.

At the end of *The Gaslight Stalker*, Esther had accepted Jack's proposal of marriage, and neither of them was prepared to wait while I took a holiday, embarked on a long gardening project, or visited my family back in the UK. They were insistent that I plan their wedding, find Esther somewhere to live after she had sold the business bequeathed to her by her doting adoptive father Isaac, and arrange some sort of employment for her while she and Jack found a house and decorated it ahead of their married life together.

But, being Esther, she couldn't leave things alone when her new employer became the victim of a particularly unpleasant campaign by those who were not prepared to allow women to improve their lot in society. And, being Jack, he couldn't allow Esther to face the danger alone, when he was a police officer dedicated to keeping the community safe. As for Uncle Percy, he was looking for another opportunity to bend the rules to breaking point in his work at Scotland Yard.

And so *The Night Caller* was not so much born as dictated by three determined characters who wouldn't leave me alone. It explores the lowly status of women generally in late Victorian society, with particular emphasis on their underlying vulnerability when they appeared to be challenging the subordinate role that male tradition had consigned to them. A generation before the strident Suffragettes with their battle banners and illegal marches, women like Esther Jacobs were being held down in their allotted places in a man's world, and brought to heel by crude physical and psychological retaliation when they attempted to push back up.

But Esther isn't easily intimidated, and she's lucky to have Jack and Percy on hand when she takes matters into her own hands, and once again requires to be rescued from the consequences of her own determination. She survives for long enough to marry her beloved Jack, but how long before she gets back into my head and demands her first child? She's already begun the campaign, and *The Prodigal Sister* will be the next in the series.

As usual, I look forward to any feedback and would be delighted if you could post a review up on **Amazon** or **Goodreads**. Or, of course, you can try the more personal approach on my website, and my Facebook page: **DavidFieldAuthor**.

Let me know what you'd like Esther and Jack to get up to next, before they take the choice out of your hands.

David

davidfieldauthor.com

Sapere Books is an exciting new publisher of brilliant fiction and popular history.

To find out more about our latest releases and our monthly bargain books visit our website: **saperebooks.com**

Made in the USA
Middletown, DE
21 March 2023

27277613R00128